The Holiday Secret

Kathryn Springer

H **HARLEQUIN**® LOVE INSPIRED®

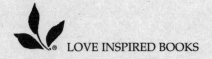

LOVE INSPIRED BOOKS

ISBN-13: 978-1-335-47947-1

The Holiday Secret

Copyright © 2019 by Kathryn Springer

www.Harlequin.com

Printed in U.S.A.

Every good gift and every perfect gift
is from above, and cometh down from the
Father of lights, with whom is no variableness,
neither shadow of turning.
—*James* 1:17

This book is lovingly dedicated to my family
for all the Christmas memories
past, present and future!

"I want your opinion on something."

Ellery tried to hide her surprise.

"I did some very last-minute Christmas shopping. This is for Bea." He withdrew a delicate silver bracelet from a box. A tiny silver horse dangled from one of the links.

"She's going to love it, Carter."

"I wanted to get Bea something just from me."

Ellery felt tears burn the backs of her eyes as Carter opened the other box.

"What do you think?"

"It's beautiful." The bracelet was similar to Bea's except for the tiny silver bell dangling from the chain.

"Anna said you can return it if you'd rather have something else," Carter said.

It took a moment for the words to register.

"This is for me?"

Carter nodded. "I thought you might like a memory, too."

"It's the wishing bell. But…you said you didn't believe that wishes can come true."

Carter smiled and slipped the bracelet over Ellery's wrist.

"I know. But lately I've been seeing more and more evidence that suggests otherwise."

Kathryn Springer is a lifelong Wisconsin resident. Growing up in a "newspaper" family, she spent long hours as a child plunking out stories on her mother's typewriter and hasn't stopped writing since. She loves to write inspirational romance because it allows her to combine her faith in God with her love of a happy ending.

Books by Kathryn Springer

Love Inspired

Castle Falls

The Bachelor Next Door
The Bachelor's Twins
The Bachelor's Perfect Match
The Holiday Secret

Mirror Lake

A Place to Call Home
Love Finds a Home
The Prodigal Comes Home
Longing for Home
The Promise of Home
Making His Way Home

Visit the Author Profile page at Harlequin.com for more titles.

Chapter One

A line from one of his daughter's favorite picture books popped into Carter Bristow's head when he rounded the corner and spotted a car parked on the side of the road.

There's something here that looks out of place.

Hmm. Tough call. Especially when Carter had to choose between a red Lexus that stood out like a cluster of winterberry against the snow-covered landscape and the woman standing next to it, pointing her cell phone at the sky.

Even with her back to him, Carter doubted she was a local. Her paper-thin leather coat and spiked-heel boots looked about as suitable for a Michigan winter as the vehicle she drove.

He pulled onto the shoulder and parked a few yards behind her. The only traffic this late in the day tended to be the four-footed kind, but Carter followed protocol and flipped on the light bar before exiting the squad car.

"Ma'am? Is everything all right?"

The woman whirled around to face him, and Carter's heart bumped against his Kevlar vest.

Definitely not a local. If they'd met before, he would have remembered. Her sleek, chin-length cap of espresso-brown hair had been strategically cut to emphasize sculpted cheekbones and a pair of eyes that Carter would have been hard-pressed to describe in a report. Not quite blue, not quite green, but a stunning combination of the two that instantly resurrected memories of the sea surrounding the Greek islands Carter had visited once while on leave.

And the flash of surprise in those eyes told Carter she hadn't realized she was no longer alone.

"I… Yes." Wind-kissed cheeks turned a deeper shade of pink. "Everything is fine, Deputy."

That ruled out engine trouble. But a young woman on a deserted stretch of road at dusk, with the snow beginning to fall as rapidly as the temperature? Not exactly Carter's definition of fine.

"Having problems with your GPS?" He turned his attention to the cell phone clutched in the woman's hand. It wouldn't be the first time Carter had stumbled upon a traveler trying to find their way out of the maze of backroads that wound through Michigan's Upper Peninsula.

"No. I was…taking a picture."

"A picture."

"Of him." She pointed to an enormous bird perched on one of the upper branches of a towering red pine.

The sight of a bald eagle surveying its kingdom was so commonplace here that Carter wouldn't have given it a second glance, let alone stop to take a photograph. It wasn't the explanation that caught him off guard, though. It was the smile that accompanied it.

Two tours in the Navy had taught Carter to look for potential danger in the most innocent of places. His brief but disastrous marriage had made him equally wary of the ones hiding behind a woman's smile.

Even a smile warm enough, bright enough, to steal some of the chill from the air.

As if aware it had drawn an audience, the eagle took

flight and performed an elegant figure-eight above their heads before it glided away.

The woman raised her cell phone again. Snapped another photo before it disappeared into the forest. "He's beautiful, isn't he?"

Beautiful.

Carter tore his gaze away, not from the eagle, but from a single gossamer snowflake that had gotten tangled in her sable lashes and cast a pointed glance at the darkening sky.

"He also knows when it's time to go home."

The smile instantly faded, but Carter refused to feel guilty for his abrupt tone—or the suggestion that she follow the eagle's example and do the same.

The individual snowflakes that appeared as harmless as thistledown were bonding together as they reached the ground, creating a thin but potentially hazardous film on the road.

Carter was nearing the end of his shift, but now he was duty-bound to make sure the woman ended up safely back on the main highway instead of in the ditch. Factor in the time he would spend entering reports and tying up the loose ends that inevitably happened at shift change and the chances of making it home before Bea's bedtime were fading as quickly as the daylight.

This impulsive photo op had put them both at risk. And all because she'd wanted to...to what? Draw a flurry of attention from her followers on social media?

Old memories rushed in, leaving a bitter taste in Carter's mouth.

His ex-wife had been the same way. Jennifer had done what she'd wanted, when she'd wanted, indifferent to the effects her decisions had on anyone else.

And if Carter was ever tempted to forget what those decisions had cost their family, all he had to do was picture the little girl patiently waiting at home for her daddy to read her a bedtime story.

The one who—thanks to the woman with the aquamarine eyes and designer sports car—would no doubt be sound asleep by the time Carter got home.

Ellery Marshall released a sigh of relief when the deputy turned left at the intersection instead of right.

For reasons Ellery couldn't quite fathom, the squad car fixed in her rearview mirror for the last twenty minutes had generated more anxiety than driving on the slick, snow-covered road.

She'd been afraid he would escort her all the way to her destination.

Ellery glanced at her GPS and sent up a silent prayer for strength as she continued on her journey.

A quick online search of places to stay in the Castle Falls area when Ellery had stopped for gas had yielded only one result. Fortunately for her, the Evergreen Inn welcomed guests year-round and everyone who'd stayed there raved about the food and warm hospitality. What no one had mentioned in their review, however, was the location.

The inn was so far off the beaten path that when Ellery finally caught a glimpse of a lamppost glowing through the heavy veil of snow, she felt like she'd emerged from the wardrobe and ended up in Narnia. The bed-and-breakfast at the end of the long driveway turned out to be just as delightful. Not the rustic lodge Ellery had been expecting to find, but a charming, two-story farmhouse built out of fieldstone. With a candle burning in each of the frost-etched windows and an oversize wreath on the door, the Evergreen could have graced the front of a Christmas card.

Ellery parked the car and tried her best to dodge the snow drifts the wind had deposited on the cobblestone path.

Should she knock? Call the number on the website?

The door swung open as Ellery was pondering the complications of showing up well after dark, suitcase in hand but without a reservation.

"Come in!" A slender woman in her midfifties, wearing a white chef's apron over jeans and a T-shirt, motioned for Ellery to come inside. "I saw the headlights when I was in the kitchen. Welcome to the Evergreen."

Ellery balked. "My boots—"

"Don't worry." The woman brushed aside Ellery's protest with a smile. "These floors have held up to Michigan winters for almost a hundred years. They can handle a little snow," she assured her. "I'm just glad you got here before the storm."

Ellery blinked.

Before the storm?

"I'm sorry for showing up this late in the evening," she murmured.

Her apology was brushed aside, too. "When you own an inn, you get used to people stopping by at all hours of the day and night." The woman extended her hand. "I'm Karen Bristow, by the way."

Ellery recognized the name from the website.

"Ellery Marshall." Ellery set her suitcase down as the innkeeper stepped behind a crescent-shaped cherry desk in the center of the lobby. "Do you have a room available?"

"I certainly do" came the cheerful response. "How many nights will you be staying with us, Miss Marshall?"

Ellery realized it was a reasonable question when one was checking into a bed-and-breakfast. If only she knew the answer.

"I... I'm not sure yet."

Karen Bristow didn't appear surprised by Ellery's vague response. "Not a problem. Even with the Countdown to Christmas starting this weekend, there are plenty of rooms available if you prefer to go day to day."

"Countdown to Christmas?" Ellery repeated.

"All the businesses in Castle Falls plan a special event on the days leading up to Christmas Eve. The official kick-off starts with a parade and the snow carnival this week-end. It's the last community-wide celebration before the town goes into hibernation." Laughter kindled in Karen Bristow's hazel-blue eyes. "Our best-kept secret isn't a secret anymore. Every year it draws more of a crowd."

Ellery couldn't tell the innkeeper that she was keep-ing a secret of her own. "I'm actually looking for...some peace and quiet."

"Well, we have plenty of that, too," the innkeeper prom-ised.

The knot in Ellery's stomach loosened a bit.

"Day to day sounds good." She reached for her purse. "I'll give you my credit card to hold the room."

"Don't worry about that now." Karen patted Ellery's hand as she fumbled with the clasp. "It's getting late and I'm sure you're tired and anxious to get settled. In the morning, I'll take you on a tour of the inn and we'll cover all the details then. How does that sound?"

Unbelievable. And...wonderful.

Because Ellery had passed "tired" a long time ago and was skidding straight toward exhaustion. Growing up, she'd stayed at some of the most exclusive hotels in the country but couldn't imagine any of them delaying the check-in process for a guest.

Ellery's grip on her purse tightened. "Thank you, Mrs. Bristow."

"Karen," the innkeeper corrected. "We have a saying here at the Evergreen. *Enter as friends, leave as family.*"

The tears that Ellery had successfully held at bay since she'd left Grand Rapids that morning banked behind her eyes. She turned and reached for her suitcase before they spilled over, only to discover someone else had already claimed possession.

"I'll carry it for you!"

The tiny bellhop standing next to Ellery's Louis Vuitton suitcase had golden-blond pigtails, Dresden-blue eyes and wore footie pajamas.

"My granddaughter, Isabella." The affection in Karen's tone belied the stern look she cast in the child's direction. "Who, I might add, is supposed to be asleep by now."

"I tried, Gramma, but my eyes wouldn't stay shut," the little girl said earnestly. "I was waiting for Daddy to get home."

For the first time, the innkeeper's smile slipped a notch. "I'm sure you'll see him bright and early tomorrow morning, sweetheart. Now, can you say hello to Miss Ellery? She just checked in."

"It's nice to meet you, Miss El'ry."

The polite greeting was accompanied by a gap-toothed grin that instantly melted Ellery's heart. "It's nice to meet you, too, Isabella."

"That's my *real* name," she was informed. "But I like Bea better 'cause that's what my daddy calls me."

Tiny, active and adorable. Ellery decided the nickname was a perfect fit.

"I almost forgot to give you this." Karen presented Ellery with an old-fashioned metal key, an accent Ellery found as delightful as the rest of the inn's decor. "You're upstairs in Wood Violet. Third door on the right—"

"Can I show Miss El'ry where it is, Gramma?" Bea interrupted, her pigtails practically vibrating with excitement. "Pleeease?"

Ellery sensed Karen's hesitation and returned the kindness the woman had extended to her. "I don't mind, but you'll have to let me carry the suitcase." She winked at Bea. "I might have brought too many shoes," she confessed in a whisper.

"Okay!"

Before Ellery could blink, the little girl had taken hold of her free hand and was towing her toward a staircase leading to the second floor. Like the rest of the lobby, the banister was dressed in twinkling lights and festive greens. A wide landing at the top, furnished with floor-to-ceiling bookcases and comfy chairs, branched off into two corridors.

Her pint-size guide pointed to the one on the left. "My room is on that side."

The comment piqued Ellery's curiosity. Karen Bristow had been the only name listed as proprietor on the inn's website. "Do your parents work here, too?"

"Just me and Daddy…when he's not at his other job." Bea skipped past several doors until they reached the one marked with a hand-painted violet. "You'll like this one because the rug is nice and squishy," she chattered on. "And there's a picture of a pony on the wall. I *love* ponies. Do you have one?"

"No." Ellery hid a smile as she set the suitcase down. "But I like them, too."

"I put one on my Christmas list," Bea whispered. "But Daddy said that Santa only has room in his sleigh for toys—"

"Bea?" Karen appeared at the top of the stairs. "Time for bed now."

Once again, Ellery found herself on the receiving end

of the child's gamine grin. "I'll see you in the morning, Miss El'ry. Gramma is making pancakes for breakfast!"

Bea skipped back down the hall, and Ellery watched Karen Bristow sweep the little girl into her arms. Heard giggles as the pair spun a graceful pirouette before disappearing through the arched doorway at the opposite end of the hall.

A familiar silence descended, pressed down on the tender places in Ellery's heart. Almost a year had gone by since her parents had passed away but it was still difficult, being alone at the end the day.

Ellery fit the key in the lock, opened the door and immediately discovered the inn's homey decor wasn't confined to the lobby downstairs.

The down comforter on the antique poster bed looked as inviting as a cloud. Thoughtful little touches—sprigs of fresh balsam tucked in a vase and a quilt folded on the chair by the corner fireplace—offered a warm welcome. Encouraged Ellery to stay awhile.

Unlike a certain county deputy.

The memory of their brief encounter made Ellery wince.

It was a little humbling to admit she'd been oblivious to the squad car—and the handsome, albeit stern-faced, deputy who'd stopped to check on her and then escorted her back to the highway.

Oh, he'd been polite. Professional. But what Ellery *hadn't* missed was the gleam of disapproval in the man's slate-gray eyes when she'd pointed out the bald eagle in the tree.

The bird *was* beautiful, but Ellery couldn't tell him that a photograph wasn't the only reason she'd stopped on the side of the road. The deputy looked like a "just the facts" type of guy. He wouldn't understand that as the number of miles to Ellery's destination had begun to diminish, the doubts had only intensified. Swirling around her, clouding her vision, like the snow that had started to fall.

The eagle had offered more than a welcome distraction. Getting out of the car for a few minutes had given her a chance to clear her head. Pray.

Because contrary to what she'd told Karen Bristow, Ellery wasn't looking for peace and quiet.

She was looking for the three brothers she hadn't known existed until yesterday.

Chapter Two

"Daddy!"

The next morning, Carter had a split second to brace himself for impact as the bedroom door flew open and a tiny missile in pink flannel hurtled toward him. "You're here!"

The guilt that had clamped around Carter's heart like a vise after Jennifer ended their marriage tightened its grip. Like the duty belt he'd been issued after accepting a job with the sheriff's department, Carter had adjusted to the added weight. If only it were as easy to set aside at the end of his shift.

He scooped Bea up in his arms, caught a whiff of something sweet. "Someone smells like maple syrup."

"Gramma is making gingerbread pancakes for Miss El'ry." Bea snuggled against his chest.

"Who?" Carter couldn't remember his mother mentioning a new guest, but with all the overtime he'd been putting in lately, it wasn't as if they'd had a lot of time to talk.

"Miss El'ry. She got here last night. I saw her out the window when I was waiting for you to come home." Bea looked up at him, all big blue eyes and rosy, sleep-flushed cheeks, not a hint of reproach on her sweet face.

Which only added another layer of guilt.

"I'm sorry, sweetheart." Carter wished he could tell Bea that he'd be there to tuck her in tonight, but past experience had taught him not to make promises he couldn't keep.

"That's aw'right. Gramma read me a bedtime story."

Carter made a mental note to thank his mom. Again. He didn't know what he'd do without her.

Transitioning from Navy SEAL to full-time deputy had been easier than taking on the role of single dad. Fortunately for him, nurturing little girls seemed to come as naturally to Karen Bristow as welcoming people into her home.

Carter didn't feel qualified for either one.

Dimpled hands patted Carter's cheeks. "We said prayers for you, too, Daddy."

He dredged up a smile. It was a good thing someone did, because prayer was beyond his skill set, too. Especially when the ones Carter had lobbed toward the heavens when he was deployed, when his marriage was falling apart, seemed to have fallen far short of their mark.

"How about you get ready for school and I'll meet you downstairs in a few minutes?" Carter tweaked Bea's button nose. "Someone has to make sure the guests don't eat all those pancakes."

"Okay!" His daughter bolted for the door the moment her feet touched the floor.

Carter finished getting ready and yanked on a pair of wool socks and hiking boots before he ventured from the room. His days of walking barefoot down to the kitchen had ended three years ago, when he'd moved back to the UP.

When it came to his daughter, though, he was willing to make some sacrifices. Living at the Evergreen gave Bea the stability she needed and Carter peace of mind.

His mom took care of Bea while he was at work and in return, Carter acted as groundskeeper and general handyman. A win-win situation for all three of them, but Carter wasn't sure he'd ever get used to strangers traipsing in and out of the house…

"Good morning!"

The middle-aged couple who greeted Carter on the landing was a perfect example. Avid cross-country skiers, they'd dressed the part in matching ski pants and softshell jackets in a blinding shade of tangerine.

"Morning." Carter paused to let the couple descend the stairs first and was about to follow when the sound of a giggle—a slightly muffled but very familiar giggle—snatched the breath from his lungs.

How many times had he warned Bea not to venture into the guest wing alone? It was the first rule Carter had established after they'd moved into the inn and one she'd never broken. Until now.

He strode toward an open door halfway down the hall, all of his focus directed on finding his daughter…

There.

In a chair by the fireplace. Dressed in her favorite red sweater and candy-cane-striped leggings. And smiling from ear to ear.

Safe.

The adrenaline surging through Carter's veins dissipated a little—until he turned his attention to the other occupant in the room.

Aquamarine eyes locked with his and Carter felt the floor shift below his feet.

No. *Way.*

"This is Miss El'ry, Daddy," Bea announced. "I gave her one of the snowflakes I made at the library."

Daddy.

The word ricocheted through Ellery's head as she stared at the man in the doorway.

But it was...*him*. The deputy she'd met on the road the night before. He'd traded his uniform for faded jeans and a long-sleeve thermal Henley, but even in casual clothes, he still managed to look intimidating.

It was the eyes, Ellery decided. Striations of silver and dark gray, the color—and temperature—of Lake Michigan during a winter storm. A muscle ticked in his jaw, the only outward sign he was as stunned as Ellery that their paths had crossed again.

She tried to push out a smile but the man's attention had already shifted back to his daughter.

"You know this side of the inn is only for the guests, Bea."

He didn't raise his voice but the girl's shoulders slumped and her sunny smile instantly disappeared. "I'm sorry, Daddy."

Given the fact this scene was unfolding in her room, Ellery decided she had the right to intervene.

"I thought it was very sweet of your daughter to bring me a welcome gift." She held up the glitter-encrusted decoration to prove that Bea had been telling the truth. "I'm Ellery Marshall, by the way."

The deputy didn't look swayed by the evidence. In fact, his grim expression was identical to the one Ellery had seen on his face the day before.

A split second of silence preceded his response. And then a measured "Carter Bristow."

"I made a snowflake for you, too, Daddy," Bea said in a small voice. "Do you want to see it?"

Carter nodded. "Of course I do. Right after breakfast."

His meaning was clear.

"Okay." Bea slid off the chair, the bounce in her step noticeably absent as she shuffled out the door.

"Please don't be upset with her," Ellery said the moment they were alone. "Bea was the one who showed me to my room last night, so I didn't think it would be a problem if I invited her in."

Ellery's explanation didn't seem to satisfy Carter Bristow. Just the opposite, in fact.

"Bea showed you to your room?"

Way to go, Elle. Now she'd probably gotten Karen Bristow in trouble, too.

It explained the innkeeper's hesitation when Ellery didn't object to Bea accompanying her upstairs. Karen knew someone who *would*.

Carter Bristow might help out at the inn, but it was obvious he didn't embrace Karen's "enter as friends, leave as family" motto.

He stepped out of the doorway and into the room, which immediately seemed to shrink in size.

"I have rules in place for Bea's protection," he said tightly, confirming her suspicions. "She doesn't always understand boundaries."

Ellery hadn't realized Carter was so tall. He was also broad in the shoulder and narrow in the waist, with a lean but muscular frame that Ellery guessed was the result of an active lifestyle, not a gym. It didn't matter that he wasn't on duty, either. Carter Bristow took command of his surroundings with an economy of words and motion.

And judging from the interaction Ellery had witnessed between father and daughter, it seemed he approached parenting in much the same way.

His *daughter*.

Ellery still couldn't believe it. There was no physical resemblance between the two that she could see. Unlike her father, there wasn't a hint of a cloud in Bea's blue eyes. Her golden hair, freed from the pigtails she'd worn the night before, had framed her heart-shaped face in a riot of loose curls. Carter's sienna-brown hair was cropped close to his head, effectively discouraging any rebellious behavior.

Ellery cast a discreet glance at Carter's left hand. No wedding ring.

What had Bea said when Ellery inquired about her family? *Just me and Daddy...*

Ellery opened her mouth, ready to apologize for her part in encouraging Isabella to break a family rule, but Carter didn't give her the opportunity.

"The main roads will be plowed and salted by checkout time," he said. "You shouldn't have any trouble getting to wherever it is you're going."

Distracted by her thoughts, and, if Ellery was completely honest, the intriguing glints of mahogany scattered throughout the grain of stubble on Carter's jaw—it took a moment for his words to register.

"I'm not checking out today."

The temperature in the room immediately dropped several degrees. "I assumed you ended up here last night because of the weather."

"No, coming to the Evergreen was always the plan." An impulsive plan. But still.

"Why?"

The blunt question caught Ellery off guard. She could only imagine how many times Carter had employed that same tactic to extract a confession from someone.

"It's the perfect place for a change of scenery, don't you agree?" Ellery said lightly. For good measure, she punctuated the question with a bright smile.

Not only did Carter Bristow *not* smile back, some undefinable emotion crackled in his eyes, there and gone as swiftly as a flash of summer lightning.

"Enjoy your stay, then."

Before Ellery could respond, he was gone. The door closed with a soft click behind him.

Ellery collapsed into the closest chair.

In spite of the fact that Carter Bristow had seemed all too ready to send her on her way—again—the urge to confide in him had been surprisingly strong.

He was a county deputy who lived five miles from Castle Falls. Wouldn't he know the people who lived in the town on a personal basis as well as a professional one?

But Ellery had already broken one of the promises she'd made to Jameson.

As if on cue, her cell began to ring.

Ellery dragged in a breath, exhaled a silent prayer for strength, and reached for her phone.

Ignoring Jameson Ford's call would only postpone the inevitable.

"I know it's early," the attorney said without preamble, "but I made some phone calls and found a private investigator who has a reputation for being thorough and discreet. I explained the situation and Dwayne Howard agreed to make the case his top priority."

Ellery's hand tightened around the phone. "That won't be necessary."

"You decided not to pursue the matter?" The relief in Jameson's voice was almost palpable. Which only made what Ellery had to admit even more difficult.

"No…because I'm already here. In Castle Falls."

Silence.

Ellery could almost *see* Jameson pacing the floor of his office the way he did the courtroom when new information called for a change in strategy.

"I thought we agreed it would be best not to rush into anything, Ellery," he finally said. "You need more facts before you let these people into your life."

By *these people*, Jameson meant the siblings that Ellery had been separated from for the past twenty-five years.

Brendan. Liam. Aiden.

Those were the signatures she'd seen on the document. Names without faces.

Brothers.

Ellery had been in Haiti, visiting one of the many orphanages the Marshall Foundation supported, when the Kane brothers had contacted the private agency that had handled her adoption. And no matter what happened in the future, Ellery's life had changed the moment Jameson had given her a copy of their letter. A piece of her past that Ellery hadn't even known was missing forty-eight hours ago.

Ordinarily, she would have taken Jameson's advice. More than a respected attorney, Jameson Ford had been her father's closest friend. But in this situation, Ellery knew she couldn't sit back and wait for a private investigator to complete an investigation.

"I don't want to read about them in a report." Ellery wanted to see where they lived.

Wanted to see *them*.

"I understand," he said. "But your parents insisted on a closed adoption to protect you. It could be they were afraid something like this would happen down the road."

A familiar ache bloomed in Ellery's chest at the mention of her parents.

She'd always known she was adopted. According to Ray and Candace Marshall, Ellery was a dream they'd carried in their hearts until the moment she'd become part of their lives. What they'd failed to reveal were the details surrounding Ellery's birth—or the fact she'd once been part of a larger family.

"I know Mom and Dad thought they were acting in my best interests at the time," Ellery said softly. "But I'm an adult now."

"Exactly," Jameson agreed. "And that's why the timing of their letter troubles me. The Kanes could have reached out to you long before now."

Before she'd inherited a sizable estate is what he really meant.

"You said that my brothers cited 'unique circumstances' when they contacted the adoption agency and asked that my records be opened," Ellery reminded him.

"That doesn't mean their motives are trustworthy," Jameson muttered.

"I appreciate your concern…but do you trust *me*?"

Jameson's sigh funneled through the speaker. "Of course I do. Most of the time you're a very levelheaded young woman."

Ellery smiled. "A levelheaded young woman with an advantage. I know my brothers' names but they don't know mine. I'll observe, not engage," she said. "You'll get a full report when I come back and we'll figure out the next step."

"You promise you won't tell anyone why you're there?"

"I promise."

"In a town that size, you won't exactly blend in."

Jameson still sounded skeptical, but Ellery sensed a softening in his attitude and pressed her advantage.

"I'm staying at an inn a few miles outside of Castle Falls," she told him. "There's a festival starting this weekend that draws people from outside the community, so I doubt anyone will notice one more visitor. It's a good plan, don't you think?"

"I think I made a mistake when I let you sit in on some of my closing arguments," Jameson retorted.

It was, Ellery knew, as close to a blessing as she would get from the attorney.

Her smile expanded to a full-blown grin.

"I'll see you soon, counselor."

Chapter Three

After dropping Bea off at school, Carter returned to the inn to get started on his to-do list.

He cut through the dining room to grab a pastry and had to duck to avoid a ball of mistletoe hanging from the chandelier. One he was sure hadn't been there the day before.

Based on past experience, Carter knew it was only the beginning. Not a single nook or cranny escaped the assault of pine garlands, twinkling lights and shiny ornaments during the month of December.

Now that Bea was old enough to help her grandmother with the annual transformation, she was all-in. A herd of plastic ponies grazed next to the sheep in the nativity set on the coffee table and Carter could barely see outside through the flurry of paper snowflakes covering the windows.

It's Jesus's birthday, Daddy. And birthdays are special.

Because the star that Carter dutifully placed on top of the tree every year wasn't half as bright as his daughter's outlook on life, he kept his feelings about Christmas to himself.

Pretended that things like peace and joy weren't far beyond his reach these days.

The double doors that separated the kitchen from the

dining room swung open and his mom breezed in. With her dark blond hair woven into a neat braid and a pristine white apron over her navy wool sweater and jeans, there was nothing pretentious about Karen Bristow.

Most of the guests didn't know that their innkeeper, who'd gained a reputation for serving mouthwatering comfort food, had studied at a prestigious culinary institute on the East Coast.

"You must be in stealth mode today," she teased. "I didn't hear you come back."

"What can I say? I take my duties as a *silent* partner very seriously," Carter said.

His mom chuckled. "The light in the atrium burned out yesterday and I couldn't find the ladder. Do you know where it is?"

As a matter of fact, Carter did. But it was safer to dodge the question than admit he'd hidden it after he'd spotted Karen teetering on the top rung, feather duster in hand, attacking a cobweb on the ceiling.

"I'll take care of it."

"Your to-do list is already a mile long," Karen said. "And this is supposed to be your day off."

"Cutting firewood is relaxing."

His mom smiled and shook her head. They'd had variations of this conversation in the past but Carter couldn't convince her that spending time outdoors, no matter what he was doing, didn't fall under the category of work.

"You skipped breakfast." Karen lifted the coffee carafe and tested its weight. "We have a new guest and I was hoping you'd have a chance to meet her before you disappeared into the woods."

"Bea already introduced us," Carter said curtly. And Ellery Marshall was the reason why he planned to stay as far away from the house as possible. "She decided to stop by Ellery's room and give her one of the snowflakes she'd made at the library."

Karen didn't appear nearly as shocked by his daughter's unsanctioned visit to the guest wing as Carter had been.

"You know Bea. No matter what craft project Maddie assigns to the children, she always makes extras to give away."

"To a woman she'd never laid eyes on before last night?"

"Ellery Marshall is close to Maddie's age and you know how much Bea likes her. Maybe that's why they bonded so quickly."

True. The local librarian and Ellery Marshall were both in their midtwenties, but as far as Carter could tell, that was the only thing the two women had in common. Maddie Montgomery had grown up in the area and her recent engagement to Aiden Kane, a man as fiercely devoted to the family business as he was to his shy fiancée, proved that Maddie was content with life in a small town.

Ellery reminded Carter of a rare butterfly that had briefly lit in Castle Falls. Looking for, in her own words, a change of scenery. And when she grew tired of the view from her upstairs window, she'd go back to where she belonged.

Like Jennifer had.

Which meant the last thing Carter wanted was for Bea to "bond" with his mother's newest guest.

"How long is she planning to stay?"

"I'm not sure," Karen admitted. "Ellery decided to go day to day."

She wouldn't even commit to an entire weekend.

The thought pushed Carter toward the door. "I'll plow the driveway before I cut wood, so if there's anything you need, let me…"

Know.

The last word got caught in Carter's throat when he spotted Ellery standing beside the desk in the lobby. It was a little unsettling to admit that a pair of ocean-blue eyes could be so…unsettling.

"You mentioned a tour…" Ellery's gaze slid back to Karen, who glided past Carter with a warm smile. "Is this a good time?"

"I have to call about a delivery, but it won't take long." Karen's smile expanded to include Carter and before she said a word, he knew his mom was about to take him up on his "if there's anything you need" offer. "I'm sure Carter won't mind taking my place. It will give you two a chance to become better acquainted."

Um. Carter did mind. A lot, actually. And he knew everything he needed to know about Ellery Marshall. But he couldn't admit that without jeopardizing the inn's five-star hospitality rating.

"Sure." He pushed the word out. "Not a problem."

"Wonderful! I'll catch up in a few minutes." Karen slipped the cell from the pocket of her apron and retreated to the kitchen to make the call.

Leaving Carter alone with Ellery for the second time that morning, the wary expression on Ellery's face a clue she wasn't looking forward to spending time with him, either.

Fine with him.

"The common areas all have names." Carter pointed at the French doors off the lobby. "That's the gathering room. Mom keeps it stocked with games and puzzles, so people like to hang out there in the evening.

"You're already familiar with the dining room, so we'll start down here." Carter strode through the lobby, bypassing both the kitchen and the parlor he'd converted into the family's private living room and opened a door at the end of the hall.

"The atrium." Carter turned and almost bumped into Ellery, who'd positioned herself in the doorway for a better look.

"I love the windows." She took a step forward and the fragrance of something exotic and floral—jasmine, maybe—teased his senses.

"You may want to come back later." Carter tried unsuccessfully to block both the scent and Ellery's attempt to enter the room. "I haven't started a fire yet and the room gets pretty cold."

Cold.

Ellery decided the description fit her tour guide, too.

Karen probably hadn't noticed the wintry look in Carter's eyes when she'd drafted him to take her place, but Ellery certainly had.

Was the man this abrupt with all the guests? Or just her?

She tried to peek around Carter, and she could almost feel his impatience as he moved to the side.

In spite of Carter's reluctance to linger any longer than was necessary, Ellery couldn't help but step into the room.

A couch upholstered in emerald-green velvet and two matching chairs curved around the hearth like a smile. A light glowed in a rustic crèche on the mantel, illuminating a small band of shepherds gathered around the holy family.

Ellery's gaze moved to the balsam tree in the corner and a lump instantly formed in her throat.

This would be her first Christmas alone.

Like Karen, Ellery's mom had decorated every room in the house. Miles of lights, rooms scented with bayberry and cloves and exquisitely wrapped gifts underneath the tree.

The month between Thanksgiving and Christmas had been filled with laughter and a steady stream of guests.

Candace Marshall had understood that entertaining was more than simply sharing the same space—it meant sharing your life.

A legacy Ellery had continued after the private plane her parents had rented had gone down on their way to a medical conference.

For the last eight months, Ellery had poured all of her time and energy into starting a foundation that bore the Marshall name. Caring for people gave her a purpose. Something that filled the empty spaces in her heart when she returned to an empty house at the end of the day.

Still… *Christmas.*

Ellery couldn't imagine celebrating the Savior's birth without her parents.

She walked across the room, each step giving her a precious moment to collect herself.

Mullioned windows framed the peaceful scene outside. When Ellery had arrived, travel weary and white-knuckled from maneuvering through the snow-covered back roads, all her attention had been focused on the inn itself, not her surroundings.

Now she could see a weathered barn and a cluster of tiny stone outbuildings with arched windows and sloping rooflines dusted with snow.

"It looks like a gingerbread village."

"I've always thought the same thing." Karen appeared at Ellery's side. "It's been suggested that I have those old buildings torn down, but I can't quite bring myself to do it yet."

"No!" The word rolled out before Ellery could stop it. "They're part of the inn's history."

"But not as practical as a parking lot," Carter interjected.

Ellery should have known. The person who'd "suggested" that Karen level the outbuildings was the same one who'd voiced his opinion on how best to utilize the empty space.

But a parking lot? Really?

Karen turned toward Carter with a smile, unaware of the tension that had been crackling in the air since the beginning of the tour. "I'll pick up Bea after school today. A package we ordered was shipped to the post office, and we can swing by to get it on our way home."

Carter shook his head. "More decorations?"

"Christmas," Karen responded cheerfully, summing up the reason for the festive environment with a single word. She winked at Ellery. "We do tend to go a little overboard this time of year."

"The tree is beautiful," Ellery murmured.

"Carter and Bea found it on the property," Karen said. "Cutting down the tree has become a tradition."

Carter cleared his throat. "And speaking of cutting down trees…"

"I believe that is my cue to take over and let my son get back to work." Karen linked her arm through Ellery's. "Carter keeps some trails open for the guests, so feel free to explore the grounds. I also have a map of cross-country ski trails near Castle Falls, if you're interested."

Ellery was interested in the people who lived there.

And more than ready to escape the chill in the air.

She could practically *feel* Carter's watchful gaze as she and Karen left the room.

"There's a full breakfast every morning, but in the winter, I discovered that people don't like to venture very far from the inn," the innkeeper told her as they retraced their steps down the hall. "You'll find a pot of homemade soup and bread in the dining room for lunch, but supper is on your own. There's also a grocery store in Castle Falls if you prefer to stash a few things in the minifridge in your room."

Karen retrieved a colorful flyer from a wire basket next to the computer and slid it across the desk. "Compliments of the Chamber of Commerce. If you decide to stay through the weekend, you might want to watch the parade." Her eyes sparkled with humor. "I can't guarantee peace and quiet, though. Most of the town shows up."

Ellery's mouth went dry.

In a small town, didn't the majority of conversations revolve around the people who lived there? If Ellery kept her eyes and ears open, it was possible she could learn more about her brothers' character from the people who saw them on a daily basis than she would from a private investigator.

Ellery studied the collage of tiny photographs on the flyer. A family sharing a picnic in a gazebo. The silhouette of a man paddling a red canoe down the river. Slices of life that made up the town her brothers called home.

"There's a calendar of events inside," Karen continued. "The Happy Cow—that's the ice cream parlor on the main street—introduces a new flavor during their open house, and that always draws a crowd. The local businesses get pretty creative."

"What do you do here, at the inn?"

"The pastor of a local church asked if I would host the live nativity this year. I've been looking for ways to connect with the community more and it seemed like the perfect opportunity..." Karen's voice trailed off and she glanced in the direction of the gathering room.

Ellery couldn't prove it, of course, but she suspected that the handsome, gray-eyed Scrooge who preferred concrete parking lots to quaint stone outbuildings didn't approve of live nativities, either.

Chapter Four

The next day, Carter spent the majority of his time in the heated garage, fixing the ancient plow that Karen had inherited when she'd bought the inn. The thing was as temperamental as an old mule, but there wasn't enough money in the budget to replace it, so Carter did his best to coax the engine to life after every snow.

On his way out, he grabbed the bucket of salt by the door. Making sure the sidewalk didn't double as a skating rink was the last item on his to-do list for the day.

A flash of color in the center of the yard caught Carter's eye and he walked over to investigate.

Bea had informed him that she was going to make a snow "horse" after school, but it had undergone a transformation since the last time Carter had seen it. The snow sculpture now boasted button eyes, a shaggy white mane recycled from the head of a dust mop and reins fashioned from a scarf that looked as if it had been spun from cotton candy.

Carter wasn't all that savvy when it came to fashion, but thanks to Jennifer's high-end taste in clothing, he could tell the difference between wool and cashmere.

Considering there were only two female guests in res-

idence at the moment, he had a pretty strong hunch who
the scarf belonged to.

How it had ended up in Bea's possession, though, was
a mystery.

In his mind's eye, Carter saw his daughter blithely skip-
ping across yet another invisible boundary. There were
two rows of hooks in the back hallway, one designated for
family and one for guests, but to a five-year-old, a scarf
was a scarf. Especially when said five-year-old was in a
hurry. Or when the article of clothing that caught her eye
happened to be in her favorite shade of pink.

Carter wasn't completely sure if either theory was correct, but there was one thing he *did* know. If he didn't re-
move the scarf before the temperature plummeted, it would
be permanently welded to Bea's snow horse come morning.

Carter's careful attempt to loosen it stirred a hint of jasmine into the night air, providing yet another clue about
the owner's identity.

The temptation to place the scarf on one of the hooks
in the hallway and go about his business was strong. But
if Bea had taken it without permission, an apology might
be in order, too.

He took the stairs two at a time to the second floor,
rapped on Ellery's door and waited. And waited some
more.

It suddenly occurred to Carter that he hadn't seen Ellery all day. A thin layer of snow still blanketed the Lexus,
which meant she hadn't driven into Castle Falls.

Feel free to explore the grounds.

His mom extended the same offer to all the guests, but
Carter couldn't imagine Ellery Marshall taking her up
on it, let alone helping herself to one of the extra pairs of
snowshoes or skis and striking out on her own.

Then again, this was the woman who'd stopped along

the road during a snowstorm to take a picture of a bald
eagle.

Karen Bristow kept a motherly eye on everyone who
stayed under her roof, so it was possible she would know
where Ellery was.

Knowing his mom usually prepped for breakfast this
time of the day, Carter retraced his steps to the first floor
and walked into the kitchen.

"Have you…" The rest of the sentence snagged in Carter's throat.

Because Ellery Marshall sat on a stool at the butcher
block island, one foot tapping to the lively beat of "Sleigh
Ride," both hands wrapped around a coffee mug.

His coffee mug.

Ellery took one look at Carter's expression and knew
there was a reason this particular room hadn't been included on her tour the day before. She wasn't supposed
to be here.

Growing up, though, the kitchen had been Ellery's
favorite room in the house. The air seasoned with her
mother's laughter, a tangle of fresh herbs in terra-cotta
pots on the windowsill and whatever soup was bubbling
away on the stove.

Even now, when she was alone, Ellery found the simple task of kneading bread dough or chopping vegetables
more relaxing than a day at the spa.

And Karen Bristow's kitchen, with its canopy of gleaming copper pots and splashes of daffodil yellow and peri-
winkle blue, had invited Ellery to linger.

Ask God to reveal what her next step should be.

No. That wasn't quite true.

What Ellery needed was the courage to *take* the next

step and actually spend some time in the town her brothers called home.

The reason she'd driven to Castle Falls in the first place.

Carter's gaze lit on the chunky ceramic mug in Ellery's hand and she made another impulsive decision.

"Would you like some coffee? I just made a fresh pot."

"There's always a coffee bar set up in the dining room," he said slowly. "My mom is pretty strict about guests wandering into the kitchen—"

"Unless that guest knows her way around a French press." Karen glided into the room, Bea bouncing along at her heels, and smiled at Ellery. "And is willing to share."

Ellery returned the woman's smile as she slipped off the stool. As tempting as it was to linger, she didn't want her presence to be a source of friction between Carter and his mother. "I'll take this upstairs to my room."

"Wait…" Carter stepped into Ellery's path. Dipped his hand into his coat pocket and produced an enormous ball of fuzzy pink yarn. "Does this belong to you?"

Bea recognized it first. "Those are Snowflake's reins, Daddy!"

"I *gave* the scarf to Bea, Deputy Bristow," Ellery said quickly, in case Carter had assumed his daughter had taken it without permission. "When we put the finishing touches on Snowflake, I was the one who suggested she needed reins."

"We?" Carter repeated.

Ellery should have known that a man trained in investigative techniques would zero in on that particular word!

Bea danced across the room and landed at Carter's feet. "Miss El'ry helped me! And tomorrow we're going to find a blanket and make Snowflake a saddle and—"

"Miss El—*Marshall*—is here on vacation," Carter interjected when Bea paused to take a breath.

"I *know* that, Daddy, but I heard her tell Gramma that she needs some peace and quiet." She looked up at him, her expression earnest. "And snow horses are very, *very* quiet."

Ellery suddenly witnessed an amazing transformation take place. A mixture of love and tenderness kindled in Carter's eyes and the corners of his lips rustled, sparking what looked to be the beginnings of an honest-to-goodness smile.

One that Ellery felt all the way down to her toes.

And if only a hint of a smile could wreak havoc with her pulse, she could only imagine what kind of lasting damage a real one would do.

"I'm sure they are." Carter scooped Bea up and parked her on the narrow ledge of his hip. "But Miss Ellery might be checking out tomorrow."

Either Karen had mentioned that Ellery's reservation was day to day or Carter had pulled up her name on the computer and done some investigating on his own.

Which reminded Ellery why she was here.

"Actually," Ellery heard herself say, "I've decided to stay a little longer."

A little longer.

What did that mean?

Two days? Three? *Ten?*

Carter didn't have a chance to ask for clarification. Because Ellery Marshall, with a smile, a graceful turn *and* his favorite coffee mug, swept out of the kitchen.

"Time to check your backpack and get ready for supper." Carter set Bea down on the floor but tiny arms clamped around his leg like a vise.

"And then we can play a game?" Bea asked hopefully. "I don't have school tomorrow."

"I think we can fit one in before bed."

Bea's grip tightened. "Are you going to be here when I wake up in the morning?"

These were the kind of questions that tore Carter up inside. "That's the plan."

A plan that was always subject to last-minute changes, but a five-year-old didn't understand the complexities of a career in law enforcement.

She released him long enough to break into a happy dance. "We can go to the parade!"

Carter had been trying *not* to think about the Christmas parade.

"Ready to beat your record?" He looked at his watch. "Ten. Nine…"

Bea squealed and shot out the door.

"I realize this time of year is…difficult," Karen said slowly, proof that no matter how skilled Carter had gotten at concealing his thoughts over the years, a mother never lost the ability to read minds.

But difficult?

Carter's lips twisted.

The word wasn't quite accurate.

Three years ago, he'd crossed multiple times zones to surprise Jennifer with what he'd thought would be the perfect Christmas gift. Spending it together as family. The first of many, because Carter had done a lot of soul-searching and decided not to reenlist.

Even half a world apart, he'd known that Jennifer was unhappy. And after Bea came along, things hadn't gotten any better. Jennifer seemed to find motherhood as difficult as marriage to a man whose career took him away for months at a time.

Carter had made a commitment to serve his country, but he'd made a commitment to his family, too. He'd applied for and accepted a job as a deputy with the sheriff's department.

Carter couldn't wait to tell Jennifer they'd be able to return to Castle Falls and start over.

Jennifer, Carter had discovered, was more than ready to start over, too. With someone else. A wealthy, jet-setting entrepreneur who'd promised Jennifer the world had proven irresistible—even if that world that didn't have room for an active toddler.

So instead of spending the holiday together, Carter had driven back to Castle Falls with a little girl who'd only seen her father twice since she'd been born. One who didn't understand that when her mother had walked away from Carter, she'd been left behind, too.

So, yeah. Christmas was tough.

"Don't you think it's time to start replacing the bad memories with some good ones?" Karen asked softly. "Not only for Bea's sake, but for your own."

She was probably right.

But the holiday that brought families together only reminded Carter that his had fallen apart.

Chapter Five

"But I want to go, Gramma!"

The tearful declaration echoed around the lobby as Ellery came down the stairs on Saturday afternoon.

Bea was looking up at her grandmother, arms crossed, her stricken expression a dramatic change from the happy little girl Ellery had spent time with over the past few days.

Ellery slowed down, unsure of what to do. She didn't want to interrupt the conversation but she didn't want it to appear like she was eavesdropping, either.

"I know you do, sweetheart, but your daddy was called in to work and I have to wait for our new guests to arrive." Karen looped her arm around her granddaughter's shoulders and gave them a comforting squeeze. "But we can still do something fun. Why don't you pick out a game and I'll make some popcorn, okay?"

"Okay." Bea's sigh stirred the wisps of golden bangs on her forehead. She trudged toward the door, feet scraping the floor with every step, so downcast she didn't notice Ellery standing at the bottom of the stairs.

Karen did. "I'm sorry, Ellery." Her smile looked a little rueful. "When there's a five-year-old in the house, life isn't always contained to the family suite."

"And it shouldn't be," Ellery said swiftly. "The inn is also your home."

"Boundaries can be tricky, though." Karen sighed. "Carter and I chose different careers but in some ways they're very similar. We're both on call 24/7. Most of the time we can make it work with some creative juggling…"

"But not today?" Ellery guessed.

Karen glanced at the doorway, making sure Bea was out of earshot.

"Carter planned to go to the parade with Bea, but his supervisor said they needed him tonight. And then fifteen minutes ago, a woman called and reserved two rooms. She guessed their party would arrive between six and eight, so I can't take his place. I realize plans change, of course, but I hate to disappoint her."

Ellery knew she might be overstepping, but it had bothered her to see Bea looking so dejected, too.

"She can go with me."

"Ellery… I can't ask you to do that," Karen protested.

"You didn't. I offered." Ellery smiled. "I enjoy Bea's company."

Karen's expression clouded suddenly, and Ellery realized the innkeeper's hesitation didn't stem from concern for her granddaughter. It was for her son.

"I don't want to put you in a difficult spot, though," Ellery said quickly. "Carter—"

"Trusts me to decide what's best for Bea when he's at work," Karen interjected firmly. "And I think that going to the parade with you this evening falls into that category."

Ellery wasn't sure he would agree, but it was too late to retract the offer. Nor did she want to.

Karen thought that Ellery was helping her, but it was the other way around.

The night she'd arrived at the inn, Ellery had been looking for a "base camp." A place to stay while she gathered information about her brothers. But God, as always, had given her so much more.

Karen's warm hospitality reminded Ellery of her mother and Bea's giggles healed the tender places in a heart still rubbed raw from grief.

"Do you want to finish getting ready while I round up Bea's snowsuit and boots and tell her the good news?" Karen asked.

Finish?

"I'm ready." Ellery paused. Glanced down at the outfit she'd chosen. "Aren't I?"

"Well…" Karen cleared her throat. "You'll be outside a few hours and the air always feels colder when you're standing in one place."

A tactful way of saying that no, she wasn't.

"I didn't think I would be spending a lot of time out-doors while I was here," Ellery admitted.

In fact, she hadn't thought much about her wardrobe at all. After Ellery made the decision to go to Castle Falls, she'd tossed a few things into her suitcase and was on the road before she could change her mind.

"No worries." The familiar twinkle stole back into Karen's eyes. "I'm sure we can find something to keep the cold at bay."

A few additional layers might insulate Ellery from the falling temperatures, but Ellery doubted they would pro-tect her from the chill in the air whenever her path crossed with Carter's.

His attitude was confusing.

But what Ellery found even *more* confusing was why it bothered her so much. Her life was complicated enough without adding Carter Bristow to the mix.

Ten minutes later, Ellery was buckling Bea into the booster seat she'd borrowed from Karen.

"Are you excited, too, Miss El'ry?" Bea piped up from the back seat.

"Yes, I am." Excited. Nervous.

Really nervous.

The butterflies that had taken up residence in Ellery's stomach after her decision to go to the parade weren't fluttering. They were performing acrobatics.

And the Lord, He is the one who goes before you. He will be with you, He will not forsake you.

The verse Ellery had leaned on, rested in, *clung to*, after her parents died rose in her mind. Calmed her heart and the butterflies.

Nothing happened that took God by surprise. No path His children walked where He wasn't at their side.

And sometimes—Ellery smiled as Bea chattered on about story time at the library—He provided another companion for the journey.

The wrinkles in the winding ribbon of road smoothed out as Ellery passed a large wooden sign that welcomed visitors to Castle Falls. A barricade across the road prevented people from continuing down the main street, but Ellery caught a glimpse of brick storefronts that gave the town an appealing turn-of-the-century feel.

Like the inn, the town was dressed in its holiday best. Strings of colorful lights graced the lampposts and fresh greenery filled the oversize planters stationed at the crosswalks, but Ellery imagined that Castle Falls would look beautiful no matter what time of the year.

She turned down a side street near the park and spotted an empty parking space. Bea bounced out of the back seat, eyes shining, and slipped her hand into Ellery's when they crossed the street.

Heads began to turn in their direction as they wove their way through the people gathered together on the sidewalk.

When Ellery assured Jameson that a lone visitor in Castle Falls wouldn't draw more than a passing glance, she hadn't considered that people would recognize Bea. And judging from the open curiosity on their faces, they were trying to figure out the connection between Ellery and a local county deputy's adorable daughter.

"I hear music, Miss El'ry!" Bea would have plunged off the curb if Ellery hadn't taken hold of her hand. "The parade is going to start!"

Ellery's heart began to thump, matching the staccato rhythm of the drums in a marching band.

Everyone's attention turned toward the music but Ellery found herself scanning the faces of the people on the opposite side of the street, looking for…strangers.

Ellery tamped down a sigh.

Everyone was a stranger.

But what did she expect? That three men she'd never laid eyes on before would be easy to spot in a crowd?

"There's Daddy!" Bea pointed a chubby finger at the squad car cruising down the street.

"I don't think…" Ellery started to say, but the words died in her throat.

Because Carter *was* leading the parade.

Carter would rather chase bad guys than be the opening act for a high school marching band decked out in fake antlers and red plastic noses.

Not that he'd been given a choice.

Carter had had no idea when he'd been called into work for a "special assignment," it would involve the annual parade. A parade Carter should have been watching from the sidelines, with Bea.

It's your hometown, Bristow, Carter's supervisor had said. *Consider it an honor.*

An honor? No. More like a punishment.

Riverside, the town's main street, was only three blocks long and yet it was crowded with moments he'd rather forget.

He'd been home on leave for the first time when he'd met travel blogger Jennifer St. John. She'd checked into the Evergreen Inn on her way to the Great Lakes Circle Tour, seeking out "backwoods beauty" on her latest adventure. To say that Carter was flattered when Jennifer had asked him to show her some of the sights around the area was an understatement.

Jennifer was stunning and vivacious—and Carter had fallen hard. In his pursuit of her attention, it didn't matter they'd been raised in different environments. Had very different goals.

Carter's mom had expressed some concerns about the relationship, but he'd brushed those aside, as well. Sure, Jennifer came from a wealthy family, but she was assertive, not entitled. Goal driven, not self-centered.

And the most amazing thing? She seemed to be wild about him, too. Delayed her trip so they could spend more time together.

Carter had been devastated when Jennifer announced it was time for her to move on. Earning a coveted spot with the SEALS meant going off the grid for months at a time, and he had no doubt there would be guys lined up to take his place at Jennifer's side.

A week before Carter was deployed again, though, she'd shown up at the inn to say goodbye. Carter's fear of losing Jennifer was stronger than any misgivings he'd had about marrying a woman he'd known less than a month. He'd stumbled through a proposal and wonder of wonders, Jennifer accepted.

It wasn't until Carter had begged her not to give up on

their marriage only a few years later that he'd found out why.

Unbeknownst to Carter, Jennifer had posted a photograph of her local "guide" on one of their outings and her popularity had skyrocketed. As she began to document their romance, her followers had clamored for more. Carter had unwittingly provided it in the form of a proposal.

Jennifer had never loved him. Not really. She'd loved what Carter had done for her career. He'd been convenient. And their child was collateral damage when Jennifer decided a family didn't fit her long-range goals.

Three-quarters of the people waving at the squad car weren't privy to all the gory details, but there was no hiding the fact Carter's marriage had crashed and burned.

One more reason he avoided the town.

You have to replace some of the bad memories with the good ones, his mom had said.

But it was difficult when the bad ones had become embedded in his heart like shrapnel.

A flurry of movement on the sidewalk caught Carter's eye.

A six-foot-tall Dalmatian wearing a gaudy plaid tuxedo was handing out candy canes along the parade route. Dash, the animal shelter's official mascot, was a fixture at events like this and never failed to attract a crowd of his own.

Carter watched Dash pause in front of an attractive young woman and two little girls. Everyone who'd turned out for the parade boasted more layers than Karen's beef Wellington, but Carter recognized Anna Leighton and her twin daughters immediately. The Leightons were the only family in town with hair the color of a newly minted penny.

Anna reached for a candy cane, but Dash was faster. In a daring move, he planted a kiss on the back of Anna's hand…and instantly blew his cover.

Liam Kane.

Carter still hadn't sent back the response card for the couple's Christmas Eve wedding. Maybe because he was still trying to figure out *why* he'd been invited.

Liam and his brothers ran Castle Falls Outfitters a few miles outside of town, but their paths hadn't crossed until Aiden, the youngest of the three, was involved in a hit-and-run.

Aiden had a reputation for being a daredevil, so his claim that a vehicle had forced him off the road had been met with skepticism in the community...and in his own family.

Carter had believed the guy, though. There were times when his own survival had been dependent on his ability to discern whether or not a person was telling the truth, and something in Aiden's story had pushed Carter to do a little more digging.

When the driver of the vehicle turned out to be the younger brother of one of the teens Aiden had been mentoring, he'd decided not to press charges.

Carter had heard that both Justin and Tim Wagner had been spending a lot of time with the Kane family since then, learning how to build canoes and maybe some valuable life skills, as well. A risky move on Aiden's part—believing in second chances—and Carter hoped the boys wouldn't take advantage of it.

His role in the case had officially ended when he'd filed his report, but apparently the Kane family thought they owed him something for doing his job. Hence the invitation to the wedding.

But as far as Carter was concerned, weddings ranked right up there with Christmas.

If it were up to him, he'd happily skip them both.

Dash moved to the next family and Carter did a double take.

The child standing next to the Leightons looked familiar, too.

Because it was *his* child...

Thank you, Mom.

Relief poured through Carter as his gaze cut to the woman standing next to Dash. He choked back a laugh.

Not only had she brought Bea to the parade, his mom must have taken his daughter's advice on what to wear for the occasion.

The knee-length down coat Karen insisted would never go out of style had, at least a decade ago. A leather bomber hat, complete with fur-lined earflaps, had been a Christmas present from Bea the previous year. The gaudy purple-and-red scarf that covered her face from nose to chin, a thank-you gift from a knitting group that had stayed at the inn.

Carter glanced in the rearview mirror just in time to see the woman standing next to Anna's twins lift her face toward the sky. The scarf slipped a few inches and Carter almost stomped on the brake, which would have made him responsible for a massive pileup of reindeer and musical instruments he would have been hard-pressed to explain to his supervisor.

Several people in the crowd shifted position, blocking Carter's view, but he knew he hadn't been imagining things. A delicate profile. A swatch of hair as dark and glossy as a coffee bean.

Ellery. Incognito.

Carter's grip tightened on the steering wheel.

Why had *she* brought Bea to the parade?

A question you'd probably know the answer to if you'd listened to your mom's voice mail, an inner voice chided.

But Carter had been helping a young mother locate the

car keys her toddler had tossed in a snowbank a few minutes before the parade started and then a guy had tried to drive around the barricade…

Now he wished he'd taken the time.

It wasn't that Carter didn't trust his mom's judgment. He did. What he *didn't* trust was the tiny spark of *something* that flickered to life whenever Ellery was nearby. Like finding an ember in the ashes of a fire you thought had been stamped out.

He'd been burned once before, though, when he'd listened to his heart and not his head.

"Look, Miss El'ry." Bea's voice dropped to an almost reverent whisper as they strolled down one of the snowy paths fanning out from the pavilion after the parade. "Ponies!"

Ellery followed the little girl's gaze to a sleigh parked under a nearby lamppost. She smiled at the description. Not ponies, but a matched pair of coal-black Friesians. The team stood shoulder to shoulder, their breath creating plumes of frost in the air. The bearded driver, clad in a buffalo-check flannel shirt and bib overalls, resembled the lumberjacks in the sepia photographs on display in Karen's gathering room.

Ellery was about to suggest they walk over and say hello, but Bea had already changed direction. Ellery's feet almost slid out from under her as she struggled to keep up.

The driver flicked the brim of his wool cap when they approached. "Good evening, ladies. Stanley Potter at your service. Are you ready for a little jaunt around the park?"

Bea clapped her hands over her mouth and the only sound that slipped out was a tiny squeak.

Ellery laughed. "I think that means yes."

"Up you go, then." Stanley held out a gloved hand and helped them onto a narrow wooden bench behind the driver's seat. "Diamond and Opal will be happy to take you on a scenic tour of the town."

He clicked his tongue and the team lurched forward, the rows of tiny silver bells attached to their leather harnesses playing a merry tune.

She studied the storefronts as the sleigh turned onto main street, hoping to see her brothers' last name on one of the signs. Ellery's brief online search before she'd left home hadn't yielded any clues as to what her brothers did for a living, nor did they show up on any of the popular social media sites.

But then again, Ellery didn't, either. Her parents had stressed the importance of connecting with people face-to-face and encouraged Ellery to do the same.

But what if there'd been more to it than that? What if they'd been afraid that her biological family would somehow find her?

Even as the thought sprang into Ellery's head, it felt like a betrayal.

Lord, I'm questioning everything these days...

"Whoa!"

Ellery grabbed Bea's hand as Stanley pulled back on the reins.

The team tossed their heads in response to the abrupt command but obeyed. The center of the street seemed like an unusual place to stop, so Ellery leaned forward.

"Is something wrong?"

"I'm not sure," came the cheerful response. "We've never been pulled over before."

Chapter Six

*P*ulled over?

Ellery twisted around. Felt her stomach drop all the way down to the toes of her boots when she saw Carter's lean frame unfold from the driver's seat of the squad car.

Karen had assured Ellery that she would let Carter know about the change in plans, but apparently, he hadn't received the memo.

Bea, whose gaze had been riveted on the horses, let out a squeal of delight when she saw the man striding toward them.

"We saw you in the parade, Daddy!" Bea said, pride shining in her eyes. "Can I go with you next time? Hannah got to ride on a float with her daddy."

"I'm afraid it's against the rules, sweetheart," Carter explained. "You have to have a badge like mine to ride in the squad car."

Bea deflated against the seat. "Okay."

Ellery saw something flash in Carter's eyes. Guilt? Regret?

Life, Ellery had learned in the past year, was too short for either one. Bea might not be able to ride in the squad car, but that didn't mean father and daughter still couldn't make another special memory.

And just like that, her mission changed.

Ellery's father, a renowned neurosurgeon, had worked long hours and been on call, too, so her parents had had to be creative and flexible when it came to spending time together. Ellery treasured those memories even more now that they were gone.

"Maybe your daddy can ride with *us* in the sleigh," she heard herself say.

Carter's expression was much easier to read this time. Disbelief.

In for a penny, in for a pound, as Ellery's mother used to say. "When are you off duty?"

"Five minutes ago," Carter admitted slowly, eyes narrowing on her face as if he was searching for an ulterior motive behind the question.

Ellery preferred to think of it as taking advantage of a memory-making opportunity.

"Mr. Stanley won't mind, Daddy!" Bea was already scooting over to make room on the bench. "It'll be fun!"

Fun looked like a completely foreign concept to the man.

"A moonlight sleigh ride with two pretty gals?" Stanley mused out loud to no one in particular. "I would call the man who gets that opportunity blessed."

Ellery could see that Carter wanted to refuse. He slid a look at Bea and that tender look—the one that told Ellery a soft heart beat behind the shield—stole into his eyes again.

"Fine. I'll park by the bank," he told Stanley. "You can pick me up over there."

The driver grinned, snapped the reins, and the sleigh glided down the street again.

Carter arrived first and Ellery felt that now-familiar uptick in her pulse at the sight of him. Like the bluffs that lined the shores of Lake Superior, there was a rugged beauty in the clash of angles and planes that made up the deputy's austere features. An appealing contrast between slate-gray eyes and sun-bronzed skin.

"Hold steady, girls!" Stanley Potter crooned at his team as Carter detached himself from the squad car and walked over to the sleigh.

Unlike Ellery and Bea, Carter didn't need any assistance. He braced his hand on the wheel and leaped lightly into the back.

Bea scooted to the end of the wooden bench and suddenly, it didn't seem nearly as roomy as it had at the start of their journey.

The warmth from Carter's body breached through the windproof outer layer of her borrowed coat and radiated against Ellery's arm. She shifted a little and the scent of his cologne, something woodsy and masculine, teased her senses.

Sooo. Maybe she hadn't thought this through.

In spite of the temperature, Ellery couldn't quite suppress a shiver. Which, of course, Carter noticed.

"Are you cold?"

"No," Ellery said quickly, holding up the ends of Karen's purple-and-red scarf as proof. "Your mom was kind enough to lend me a few things."

Carter flicked a look at the gold bells threaded through the tassels. "I'm not sure I'd call that kind," he murmured.

Ellery's lips parted in shock. Had the taciturn deputy actually cracked a *joke*?

Her gaze flew to meet his and the gleam of laughter in Carter's eyes was like finding an agate on the Lake Superior shoreline. She wanted more.

"It's warm. And…" Ellery paused, searching for the right word. "Warm."

Carter's lips twitched at the corners. "Like the hat?" He tugged on one of the earflaps and in the process, his fingers accidentally grazed the curve of Ellery's jaw.

The featherlight touch triggered a flash of heat that streaked through Ellery and spilled into her cheeks.

Carter's hand dropped to his side and Ellery heard him suck in a quiet breath, as if he'd felt it, too.

"Is everyone ready?" Stanley called out, breaking the fragile connection between them.

Sixty seconds ago, Ellery would have said yes. Now she wasn't so sure.

Fortunately, Stanley didn't wait for an answer. He whistled and Diamond and Opal lurched forward down the snow-covered street.

Carter had scaled mountains. Jumped from a helicopter into the ocean. Hiked through deserts hot enough to melt the top layer of a man's skin.

But never had Carter felt more out of his element than he did right now, in a sleigh drawn by two horses that jingled all the way down the main street.

Everything was out of his control. The speed. The route.

The clatter of his pulse when Ellery smiled at a group of teenagers who waved as the sleigh glided past them.

This is for Bea, Carter reminded himself. The last thing he wanted to do was disappoint her again, even if it meant a forced trip down Memory Lane.

He shot a sideways glance at Ellery. She looked as captivated by the passing scenery as his daughter and Carter's lips twisted.

His ex-wife had been fascinated with Castle Falls's small-town charm, too, but in her case, the feeling hadn't lasted very long. Shortly after Carter was deployed again, the woman who'd claimed she wanted to experience everything the area had to offer quickly ran out of things to do.

The sleigh turned at the corner and their driver pointed

to a grove of trees. "The stone arch you see over there is a local landmark. Folks around here call it the wishing bell."

Bea wriggled closer to the side of the sleigh, trying to get a better look. "Why?"

"I'm not from around here, mind you, but I was told that if you make a wish and the bell rings, it will come true. Did I get that right, Deputy?"

The part about it being a local landmark, yes. The rest of the story, of course, was pure fantasy. Probably something the Chamber of Commerce had cooked up for tourists back in the day. The arch not only provided a pretty backdrop for photos, it also happened to be a stone's throw away from the businesses that kept the town alive.

If Carter said that, though, he'd be guilty of letting his cynicism show, so he settled for a safe "That's what I've heard," instead.

Bea clapped her hands together and before she said a word, Carter knew what was coming next. "Let's make a wish, Daddy!"

"I wish I had some of the caramel corn I saw for sale in the park," Carter said promptly. "And listen." He put his finger to his lips. "Bells."

Yes, the sound was coming from the ones sewn on the horses' harnesses. And yes, it was a blatant attempt to avoid the very place Carter had declared his love to Jennifer. But thankfully, it worked.

"I hear them!" Bea nodded so vigorously that her hat almost slipped off her head.

Stanley laughed. "I'll let you off at the next stop, then." He guided the horses to the side of the street and shouted another "whoa" that caught the attention of a group of prospective passengers.

Carter hopped out first. Bea launched herself into his arms and Carter set her on the ground before turning his attention to Ellery. The bulky coat and miles of scarf hampered her movements as she attempted to climb down.

Carter automatically reached for her, too. His hands bracketed Ellery's trim waist and he lifted her down. The fur-lined flaps of the bomber hat obscured her expression, but Carter heard a slight gasp as her feet touched the ground.

"Okay?"

"Y-yes."

That made one of them, anyway.

Carter was still battling another unexpected spark of attraction before it gained more ground.

"Hold on, sweetheart. Your boot came untied." Ellery dropped to her knees in the snow and Bea stood patiently while she tightened the laces. When Ellery finished, Bea hooked her arms around Ellery's slender waist and gave her a hug, a gesture of affection so unaffected that it caused Carter's breath to seize in his lungs.

This couldn't happen.

Carter wouldn't *let* it happen.

He hadn't dated anyone since the divorce. By choice. It had taken months for Bea to emerge from her shell after Jennifer abandoned them. To find her smile again. It was too risky to open a door that could potentially lead to more hurt. Protecting his daughter was Carter's first priority.

If he did decide to wade into the dating pool again, it would be with a local girl. Someone who wouldn't miss the theater and concerts and stores that stayed open past five.

He appreciated the fact that Ellery had brought Bea to the parade, but she had no ties to the area. He didn't want to risk getting attached— Carter caught himself. He didn't want *Bea* to get attached to Ellery.

He tucked a folded bill into the wool cap that now lay upside down on the seat and looked around for Bea. Just as he suspected, she was deep in conversation with the horses. One small hand clutched Ellery's while she stroked their velvety noses with the other.

Carter cleared his throat. "Ready to go, Bea?"

She nodded, her eyes shining. "I'm saying goodbye to the ponies!"

"And what do you say to Mr. Stanley?" Carter prompted.

"Thank you!" Bea blew kisses at the horses before she skipped back to his side.

"The caramel corn stand is by the pavilion." Carter didn't have time to gauge the fastest way to get there. Bea grabbed his hand, too, linking the three of them together.

If that wasn't bad enough, it suddenly occurred to Carter that his brilliant plan to exchange a trip to the wishing bell for the caramel corn stand meant taking a path through the center of the park.

Luminaries made from blocks of ice lined the pathways that meandered through the park. Snow continued to fall, the kind that covered everything with a sparkling crystal veneer.

Local organizations and vendors had painted their booths to look like gingerbread houses, each one with a different theme. And all of them more tempting to a five-year-old than the candy display in the checkout line of the grocery store.

The idea for the Countdown to Christmas had been sown during a Chamber of Commerce meeting, but every year the event grew in popularity…and size.

Members of the historical society, dressed in clothing that looked as if they'd stepped from a photograph on the wall of the museum, strolled through the park singing Christmas carols. Food booths and carnival-type games supervised by what looked to be an entire squadron of Santa's elves encouraged people to linger a while.

"Can we play some games, too?" Bea pointed to a boy about her age, rolling a soccer ball toward a cluster of red-and-white-striped bowling pins.

"Of course," Ellery said before Carter had a chance to respond.

Bea could hardly contain her excitement. The teenage volunteer, another one of Santa's friendly elves, looked at Carter when they reached the front of the line.

"Ready to try snow bowling?" she asked cheerfully.

"Yes." Once again, Ellery beat him to the verbal punch. "We'll need three snowballs."

Carter raised a brow when the teen handed each of them a soccer ball. "Snowballs?"

"Use your imagination," Ellery whispered.

For a man who'd been through what Carter had, imagination ranked right up there with dreams.

Both of them led to disappointment.

Bea rolled the ball and knocked down two candy canes. Ellery missed them all by a mile, but she tossed a teasing smile at Carter when it was his turn.

"Don't worry, Deputy. You can do it."

Ordinarily, Ellery would have been right.

But there was nothing ordinary about the way the evening was playing out.

Carter had been one of the best marksmen in his unit, but now he wasn't as confident of his skills. Not when the scent of jasmine—and Ellery's smile—were wreaking havoc with his concentration.

Somehow, whether driven by desperation or determination, Carter's survival skills kicked into gear again. He managed to knock all five candy canes down. The "elf" awarded him with a stuffed polar bear that he promptly turned over to Bea.

By the time Carter spotted the caramel corn booth, he

had played pin the carrot nose on the snowman and decorated a sugar cookie. The second activity took longer than it should have because Ellery and Bea applied frosting and sprinkles with the same amount of care Michelangelo must have used when painting the Sistine Chapel.

"You spent fifteen minutes decorating a cookie that will be gone in fifteen seconds," Carter said as they walked away.

The tip of Ellery's tongue swept away a sprinkle clinging to the corner of her mouth. "Your point?"

Ah…he'd *had* a point.

He just couldn't remember what it was at the moment.

Carter dragged his gaze away from Ellery's lips and focused his attention on the booth at the end of the path.

The woman behind the counter wore a white wig, oversize spectacles and a red velvet coat, but Carter recognized Sunni Mason.

Before he could greet her by name, though, Sunni tapped the badge hanging from a red-and-white lanyard around her neck.

"Mrs. Paws," he read out loud.

"That's right." She grinned. "Now, which flavor of popcorn would you like? Caramel or white chocolate?"

Carter glanced down at his daughter. "Bea?"

She wasn't looking at Sunni or the bags of mouthwatering caramel corn lined up on the counter. Something *inside* the booth had claimed her attention.

A dog, curled up on a fleece blanket not far from Sunni's feet.

And in spite of the festive red-and-green bandanna knotted around the animal's neck, Carter recognized him, too.

Bea's arms clamped around his leg when the dog's lips peeled back, exposing a row of jagged teeth.

"Don't worry. That's just Dodger's way of smiling at you," Sunni explained. She slipped her hand into the pocket of her apron and pulled out a biscuit. "Would you like to give him a treat?"

Bea's eyes lit up. "Uh-huh." She dropped to her knees and giggled when the dog licked her face instead of the biscuit. "He likes me!"

"Of course he does. Dodger might not look like a show dog but he has a very big heart." Sunni dropped her voice a notch. "In fact, if it wasn't for your daddy, I'm not sure where he would be now."

"My daddy?" Bea breathed.

"That's right. Dodger got lost in the woods and he was hurt. Deputy Bristow—your daddy—saved his life."

"I *found* him," Carter corrected.

"And brought him to the vet. And, if the rumors are true, paid his bills."

Were veterinarians exempt from patient confidentiality? Carter made a mental note to find out.

"Not that big of a deal," he muttered.

"I don't agree." Sunni looked at Bea. "Your daddy is a hero and I'm sure Dodger thinks so, too."

Bitterness rose in Carter's throat, leaving a sour taste in his mouth.

In spite of what Sunni claimed, he wasn't a hero. Not when he hadn't been able to save his own marriage.

Carter bared his teeth in a smile. "Just doing my job."

"Dodger likes Miss El'ry, too."

Sunni looked a little startled when Bea knelt down beside Ellery. She must have assumed that Ellery was the next customer in line.

And the flash of delight Carter saw on the woman's face told him that she'd just made another one.

"I'm sorry. I didn't realize you were together."

Chapter Seven

Ellery found herself on the receiving end of a wide smile. And there was no mistaking the slight emphasis the dog's owner had put on the last word.

Togeth— No.

Oh, no.

In spite of the temperature, heat flooded Ellery's cheeks. She didn't dare look at Carter. "I'm a guest…at the inn."

"Then welcome to our town!" The woman's smile spilled into the lines fanning out from her chocolate-brown eyes. "What brings you to Castle Falls?"

Ellery caught her lower lip between her teeth. She didn't want to lie but she couldn't tell the truth, either. *Observe, not engage.* What she'd thought would be a simple strategy had become more complicated since she'd arrived.

Bea—bless her heart—answered the question Ellery couldn't.

"Miss El'ry needs peace and quiet," she said.

The woman chuckled. "You'll find plenty of that around here," she affirmed, echoing what Karen had said the day Ellery checked into the inn. "Where do you call home?"

"Downstate…" Relief poured through Ellery when three small children scampered up to the booth, their parents a few steps behind. Ellery moved aside to make room and put some distance between herself and the woman's curiosity.

Carter scooped Bea up in his arms. "It's almost bedtime, Issybea. You can pick one more thing to do before Miss Ellery takes you home."

Bea didn't have to think about it. "The snow maze!"

Ellery pressed her lips together to seal off a smile.

Carter's adorable, precocious daughter had chosen the activity guaranteed to postpone bedtime a little bit longer. It was clear Carter knew he'd been outmaneuvered by a five-year-old, but the look he leveled at Ellery said he held her partially responsible for the decision.

"It starts over there," she said helpfully. "At the North Pole."

Carter set Bea down and gestured toward the booth flanked by two gigantic candy canes. "Lead the way."

One of the elves—a lanky teenage boy wearing pointed ears and a ball cap emblazoned with the words Team Santa—greeted them at the entrance of the maze. He handed out plastic tokens shaped like snowflakes to each of them and winked at Bea.

"Don't lose this. You'll need it when you get to the end."

Carter examined his snowflake with the same intensity he would devote to a piece of evidence but Bea didn't display any of her father's skepticism. She skipped ahead of them and disappeared into the maze, leaving Carter and Ellery with no choice but to follow.

The walls, built from blocks of snow, were high enough that Ellery couldn't see over the top. Bea led the way and giggled when the first turn led them to a dead end. They retraced their steps and waited while she chose another path.

"This is amazing," Ellery whispered. "Does the Chamber of Commerce do this every year?"

"I have no idea," Carter admitted. "I haven't been to one of these events since…my last deployment."

Ellery shouldn't have been surprised to learn Carter had been in the military. "Which branch?"

"Navy," he said curtly. "Special forces."

He'd been a *SEAL*?

A dozen questions sprang into Ellery's mind, but she remained silent, afraid that if she delved into Carter's personal life, it would give him license to do the same with hers.

Not that he seemed interested in finding out more about her. Ellery got the feeling Carter had already formed an opinion of her and for reasons she didn't quite understand, it wasn't very favorable.

Bea, who'd been zipping through the icy corridors as quickly as her namesake, disappeared around a corner.

"I think *she* needs a scarf with bells." Carter quickened his pace to catch up with her, but not before Ellery saw the telltale glint in his eyes.

Two jokes in the space of an hour. The man did have a sense of humor—and it looked really good on him…

Carter stopped so abruptly that Ellery almost crashed into him.

They'd reached the end of the maze. Ellery peeked over Carter's shoulder and she spotted the landmark Stanley Potter had pointed out during their tour. Only now she could see a copper bell hanging from the center of a stone arch. Dozens of plastic snowflakes were scattered on and around the rustic bench beneath it.

"Look, Daddy! The wishing bell!" Bea danced ahead of them. "Come on!"

Ellery took a step forward, but Carter didn't budge. His eyes remained riveted on Bea as she closed her eyes and pressed the snowflake against her heart.

"Why do people encourage things like this?" he murmured.

"Things like what?"

"Wishes."

The muscle working in Carter's jaw told Ellery he wasn't kidding. She also realized he wasn't expecting an answer, but the words slipped from her lips before she could stop them.

"Because they remind us of what's important?"

Carter cut a sharp, disbelieving glance in her direction.

"There's no wind. Bea is going to be disappointed when that silly bell doesn't ring after she makes a wish."

"Bea is five years old," Ellery said softly. "She'll make another one the next time you bring her. I'm sure you've made a wish when you've blown out the candles on your birthday cake or seen a falling star. It's not so much about the wish coming true…it's about *hope*."

Carter didn't respond and Ellery was afraid he didn't believe in that, either.

Ellery closed her eyes, exchanging the wish for a prayer.

Only this time, it wasn't for the family she'd come to Castle Falls to find.

It was for Carter's.

Carter let himself into the back hallway and hung his coat on the wooden rack by the door. One hook over, the scarf Ellery had borrowed from his mom cascaded down the wall and formed a red-and-purple puddle on the floor.

A smile worked its way free before Carter realized what was happening.

Another sneak attack.

Just when he thought Ellery was cut from the same designer fabric as his ex-wife, who wouldn't have been caught dead in a borrowed ensemble, she did something that took Carter by surprise.

But being a good cop meant reducing the element of surprise.

Because surprises could be dangerous. Change a man's life.

Like the soft chime of a bell on a windless night.

Did you hear that, Daddy?

Bea had breathed the words as they'd stepped back into the maze, her eyes filled with wonder.

Carter had heard it, all right. But he sure couldn't explain it.

The words Ellery had spoken circled back through his mind.

It's hope.

Maybe the most dangerous thing of all.

Carter took the back staircase to the second floor, locked up his duty weapon and changed out of his uniform before stopping in to check on Bea.

Tiny lights in every color of the rainbow decorated the branches of a small artificial tree in the corner. Christmas had sneaked in here, too.

He stepped over a miniature horse corral spread out on the rug and leaned down, pressed a kiss against Bea's forehead. Her eyes flickered open.

She smiled and burrowed deeper under the comforter. "'Night, Daddy. Wasn't it fun?"

"Yes." Inexplicably, Carter's throat tightened.

Most of the time, his mom supervised Bea's activities and outings. Carter heard about their adventures secondhand. His mom easily navigated the carefree, glitter-strewn world of a little girl. Understood the importance of hair bows and tea parties and books with ponies prancing on the cover.

Carefree wasn't exactly a word in Carter's vocabulary anymore. Protecting and serving defined his days. The very nature of his career required that he remain vigilant. The same things that made Carter a good officer made it hard for him to let his guard down. But if he were completely honest, he had enjoyed the evening.

Seeing his daughter happy made Carter happy.

But that still didn't mean it was in Bea's best interests to spend time with Ellery.

"See you in the morning, sweetheart." Carter turned off the nightlight and backed out of the room.

There was no sign of his mom, but if new guests had arrived in the past few hours, chances were strong that Karen would be in the kitchen, starting the breakfast prep work.

Carter found her at the butcher block island, up to her elbows in bread dough.

"Mom—"

"I know what you're going to say. And I'm sorry if you're upset that I let Bea go to the parade tonight," she said quietly. "Ellery overheard me telling Bea that I had to be here when the guests arrived. She saw how disappointed Bea was and offered to take her along."

"I'm not upset." Carter blew out a sigh. "And I do trust your judgment. But it doesn't make sense to me that someone who claims she came here for peace and quiet extended the invitation to a five-year-old who doesn't stop talking even when she's asleep."

Karen smiled at the description. "I know your job has made you a little…suspicious of people's motives, but I don't see anything in Ellery that raises a red flag."

Carter did.

"I don't want Bea to be a…a cure for boredom, that's all. She isn't a doll that Ellery Marshall can discard when she gets tired of playing with her."

Understanding dawned in his mom's eyes.

"Carter." A quiet exhale stirred the silence in the room. "Please tell me that you aren't comparing Ellery to Jennifer."

"They seem to have a lot in common," he said tightly. "You saw the car she drives. The clothes she wears."

"Yes, but those kinds of things aren't an accurate gauge of what's in a person's heart," Karen protested. "You have to look beyond them."

Carter knew she was right.

But the plain and simple truth?

He was afraid to take his mom's advice.

Afraid that if he did, he'd discover that Ellery was as beautiful on the inside as she was in her borrowed red-and-purple scarf and fur-trimmed hat.

Because it wouldn't change the fact that her stay in Castle Falls would be over as quickly as Bea unwrapped her presents on Christmas morning.

Chapter Eight

Sunday morning, Ellery woke up to the aroma of freshly baked bread and the insistent hum of her cell phone on the nightstand next to the bed.

She pushed her hair out of her eyes and reached for it. Groaned when she saw the time…and the name flashing on the screen.

Jameson.

"Good morning!" Ellery injected what she hoped was the right amount of enthusiasm into her tone. "How are you?"

"When are you coming home?" The attorney parried, making it clear that his answer was dependent on her response.

Ellery flopped onto her back and stared at the tiny glass prisms hanging from the antique chandelier on the ceiling. "I'm not sure," she hedged.

"I'm trying to see things from your perspective, Elle, but I'm still not entirely sure what it is you're hoping to accomplish."

"I don't know if I can explain it, either," Ellery murmured. "It's…complicated."

"Have you had an opportunity to explore Castle Falls?"

"Last night." Ellery was glad that Jameson couldn't see the wave of color that heated her cheeks.

In addition to the tangle of emotions Ellery had been sorting through upon discovering she had brothers, now she was dealing with those that Carter stirred inside her.

"I'm still not comfortable with this, Ellery. One phone call to Dwayne Howard and we'll have everything we need to know about the Kanes."

That was the trouble. If Ellery agreed, she suspected the private investigator and Jameson would decide what was important.

And even though Ellery hadn't discovered anything about her brothers, how could she explain that being in Castle Falls made her feel closer to them somehow? Knowing she was part of a family—even one she hadn't met yet—eased some of the emptiness inside.

So did spending time with Bea.

And Carter, an inner voice teased.

Ellery tried to sweep the thought away, only to discover every moment of their evening together had become woven into her memory.

The sense of humor lurking behind the man's serious, just-the-facts exterior intrigued her. The patience and tenderness he displayed with Bea tugged at her heart.

Not to mention that Carter was a former Navy SEAL who'd rescued an abandoned dog and paid its vet bills...

"I'm not ready to leave yet."

When Jameson sighed, Ellery realized she'd said the words out loud.

"All right," he said. "I'll be tied up with a jury trial for a few days, but you'll keep me in the loop."

It wasn't posed in the form of a question but Ellery didn't take offense. The attorney had been a steadfast presence after her parents died and Ellery knew Jameson's command stemmed from concern, not a need to control.

"Of course I will. And you have to agree to keep the private investigator on hold until I get back," Ellery said.

"I… I'm sorry, Elle." She heard a sudden commotion in the background. "I have to run."

"Bye, Jameson." Ellery was glad he couldn't see the look of relief on her face right before she hung up the phone.

There was no use trying to fall back to sleep. If Jameson's phone call hadn't awakened her, the enticing aromas seeping through the vents in the floor would have done the trick.

Ellery took a quick shower, pulled on a cashmere tunic in her favorite shade of robin's-egg blue, black leggings and ballet flats before padding downstairs.

She expected to find the dining room empty, but Karen and Carter were standing in front of the beverage table, deep in conversation.

A *tense* conversation, judging from their expressions.

"I'm sorry." Ellery pulled up short. "I didn't mean to interrupt."

Karen waved aside her apology.

"I'm glad you did," the innkeeper said candidly. "Carter and I were having a difference of opinion and now I can call an official time-out."

Ellery stifled a groan. One more thing the man could hold against her!

"The only reason you want to call a time-out is because your argument isn't holding up," Carter retorted.

"This isn't court, Deputy Bristow." Karen winked at Ellery as she poured a third cup of coffee. "The director of the local shelter called a few minutes ago and asked if I'd be willing to foster one of their animals."

"And you don't allow pets at the inn," Ellery guessed.

Carter shot Karen a dark look. "Yes, but in this situation, Mom is willing to bend the rules."

"That's because the animal is a horse and it won't be inside." Karen's eyes twinkled. "Technically, I'm not bending the rule because it doesn't apply.

"The horse's owner is moving into an assisted living facility and no one in his family has a place for it. They found a summer camp downstate that accepts older horses for a therapeutic riding program, but the entire staff gets time off in December, so it needs a temporary home. I'm one of the few people in the area who has a barn."

"You also have an inn to run." Carter pointed to the chalkboard calendar. "And a to-do list that literally takes up an entire wall."

"Volunteers from the shelter will come out here every other day to take the horse out for some exercise. Clean out its stall." Karen chuckled. "The only thing I have to do is figure out how to convince Bea that she won't be able to sleep in the barn."

"She'll be over the moon." An image of Bea's reaction when she'd spotted the sleigh brought a smile to Ellery's face. "I've never seen a girl who loves horses more than Bea."

"Thank you for voting in my favor, Ellery." Carter grabbed his coffee mug. "Now, if you'll both excuse me, I have to check on Bea and finish getting ready for work."

The moment they were alone, Ellery turned to Karen.

"I said that Bea loves horses. How is that voting in his favor?"

Karen's face clouded. "Because Carter is afraid Bea will form an attachment to something and then get hurt when it's time to say goodbye."

"But if a person closes himself off like that, he'll miss out on the good things, too," Ellery protested.

"I agree. Carter will leave the final decision up to me, but there's a reason why he is protective. There was a time when he…couldn't be there for Bea and I believe he's trying to make up for it."

Ellery felt a tug on her heart. "It must be difficult when servicemen and women are away from home when something bad happens. How…how long ago did Bea's mother pass away?"

Karen appeared shocked by the question. "Carter isn't a widower," she said after a moment. "Jennifer is alive and well and, from what I've heard, still jet-setting around the world. She walked out on Carter and Bea three years ago and never looked back."

Carter's ex-wife had *abandoned* her family?

Ellery could hardly comprehend it.

"That must have been devastating."

A shadow darkened Karen's eyes. "Carter blamed himself and I think he still carries a lot of guilt."

Remembering their conversation at the wishing bell the night before, Ellery had another theory. It was more than what Carter carried. It was what he'd lost.

Hope.

Carter closed Bea's bedroom door and backed into the hallway, careful not to disturb her.

Even on the days she didn't attend kindergarten, Bea was up with the sunrise, but this time, she hadn't even stirred.

Apparently, his little girl needed some extra sleep to recharge her batteries after last night's outing. What Carter needed was another cup of java before he started his shift.

And one more opportunity to talk some sense into his mom.

He couldn't believe she was actually contemplating the idea of fostering an animal.

We have the space, Carter. It does seem like the perfect solution, Karen had said reasonably.

The perfect solution for Sunni Mason. But all Carter could see was a fifteen-hundred-pound problem.

He cut through the dining room on his way to the kitchen, expecting to see Ellery enjoying breakfast with the new guests.

But no, she was gliding between the table with a coffee carafe. Wearing a bright smile and one of the white aprons his mom kept on peg behind the door.

"These are the best popovers I've ever tasted," one of the women declared. "Will you share the recipe?"

"I'll talk to the chef and see what I can do," Ellery promised before disappearing into the kitchen again.

She wasn't supposed to *be* in the kitchen.

Or his thoughts.

But lately, Carter hadn't been very successful at keeping Ellery out of either one.

He cut between the tables and found Ellery standing beside Karen at the butcher block island, working in tandem as they plated the main entrée.

Jennifer hadn't stepped foot in the kitchen after the wedding and acted more like a paying guest than family. Carter had expected his mom and Jennifer would become close over time, but a month after his deployment, Jennifer had packed up her things and moved back to Chicago.

And yet somehow, in the space of a few days, Ellery Marshall had managed to charm her way into the hearts of both the women in Carter's life.

"I never would have thought of using cranberries and fresh rosemary as a garnish." Karen looked down at Ellery's handiwork and grinned. "It looks like a Christmas wreath."

Ellery stared down at the tray as if she hadn't realized what she'd done. "I'm sorry…"

"Don't you dare apologize!" Karen cut off her apology. "I love it." She added a sprig of rosemary to the plate. "I'm beginning to think you're an undercover restaurant critic or a reporter who wants to write about the inn and make us famous," she teased. "'Fess up, Ellery. What's the real reason you're here in Castle Falls?"

Carter shifted his weight and the floorboards creaked, giving his position away. Ellery's head snapped up. In that brief, unguarded moment, Carter saw something in her eyes that he recognized.

Guilt.

Ellery covered it with a smile but the tense set of her shoulders, the way she averted her gaze, set off Carter's inner alarm system as she picked up the tray.

"I'll take this out." Ellery slipped past Carter but he followed her back to the dining room.

Was she avoiding the question? Or him?

"I've got it from here." Carter relieved Ellery of her burden. He didn't typically serve the guests while in uniform, but it wasn't Ellery's job to serve them at all.

Someone had to follow the rules.

"Thank you." A man sitting with his wife at a corner table thrust out his hand after Carter set the plates down. "And be careful out there, Deputy."

Out of the corner of his eye, Carter saw Ellery disappear through the doorway that led to the lobby.

"I will," Carter murmured.

He wondered what the man would think if Carter admitted that the slender woman who'd poured their coffee a few minutes ago was more dangerous than any criminals he might encounter during his shift? At least when it came to Carter's peace of mind.

Chapter Nine

Snow crunched underneath Ellery's feet as she hiked between the tidy rows of apple trees on Monday afternoon, the bells on her scarf tinkling like miniature wind chimes.

It was the first time she'd explored the grounds since her arrival, but the old orchard visible from the upstairs window had beckoned to her.

Karen had left to pick up Bea from school shortly before Ellery set out on her walk, leaving her alone with her thoughts.

After Ellery had stumbled into the middle of Carter and Karen's "discussion" the day before, she'd spent the remainder of the day in her room, sifting through some old issues of the local newspaper with the hope of finding a mention of her brothers.

And avoiding Carter in the process.

Once again, with a frequency that was starting to concern her, Ellery's thoughts returned to a handsome deputy.

Jennifer is alive and well and, from what I've heard, still jet-setting around the world. She walked out on Carter and Bea three years ago and never looked back.

Ellery didn't know why she'd assumed that Carter's wife had passed away. Maybe because it had never crossed her mind that a woman would simply walk away from her husband and child.

Ellery was well acquainted with grief. Knew that losing a person you loved changed the landscape of your life forever. But if that person *chose* to leave... Was it any wonder the walls around Carter's heart were as impenetrable as his bulletproof vest?

Karen had said that Carter had moved back to Castle Falls three years ago. Bea would have been a toddler at the time. Did she even remember her mother?

Ellery wasn't naive enough to believe that every marriage was as idyllic as her parents', but she couldn't imagine a woman completing severing ties with her child.

The sound of laughter interrupted Ellery's thoughts and when she followed it to its source, spotted a pickup truck and trailer parked near the barn.

The inn's four-legged guest had arrived.

Karen stood outside with Bea, chatting with a woman Ellery instantly recognized from one of the booths they'd visited after the parade. Only today she wore a stocking cap instead of a white wig and had traded her red velvet coat for a more practical one made of fleece.

Ellery waved as she cut across the yard, but Bea intercepted her before she reached the door.

"We've got a pony, Miss El'ry!" she shouted. "And it looks just like Snowflake! Come see!"

Bea slipped her hand into Ellery's and tugged her toward the barn.

Ellery laughed as snow sifted over the tops of her boots. The sound caught the attention of Karen and her companion. Both women turned toward her with a smile.

"Ellery, this is Sunni Mason." Karen made the introductions. "The president of the animal shelter's volunteer board. Sunni, Ellery Marshall. Ellery is a guest but she's been so helpful, I'm beginning to think she's an answer to prayer."

"Ellery and I met on Saturday night, when I was dressed up as Mrs. Paws." Sunni's eyes twinkled. "Carter and Ellery and Isabella stopped by the animal shelter's booth and it looked like they were all having a wonderful time."

"Carter didn't mention he'd met up with you and Bea." Karen looked astonished—not to mention a little intrigued—by the information.

Uh-oh.

"I enjoy Bea's company." Ellery smiled down at the girl. She didn't want Carter's mother questioning her relationship with Carter, too.

Because there *was* no relationship.

"We went on a sleigh ride," Bea said. "And Daddy played games with us, didn't he, Miss El'ry?"

"A sleigh ride," Karen repeated. "And…games?"

Ellery nodded.

Fortunately, she was saved from having to answer more questions about the evening when a series of loud thumps drew everyone's attention to the barn.

"We're waiting until my boys get Sugar settled into her new home before we go inside," Sunni said.

Bea's shoulders rolled with her sigh. "It's taking a looong time."

More thumps…and a muffled groan.

Sunni and Karen exchanged a wide-eyed look over Bea's head.

"How about I take a quick peek inside and see how they're doing?" Ellery offered quickly. "I used to do a fair amount of riding when I was younger."

"Fine by me," Sunni said. "Sugar is a tad…um…bigger than the animals we usually deal with at the shelter."

Ellery stepped into the barn and the first thing she saw

was the broomstick tail of an enormous white horse blocking the narrow aisle that bisected the building.

Ellery couldn't see anyone, but she could hear an animated conversation taking place on the opposite end of the barn.

"You're the one who claimed that putting a horse in a stall would be as easy as steering a canoe," a masculine voice grumbled.

"My canoe doesn't have a mind of its own…and the, um, stern isn't nearly as wide" came the swift retort.

"Try to lure her inside with the apple we brought along." A third person joined the conversation.

A moment of silence. And then, "That was for the horse?"

"Seriously?" A huff of frustration echoed through the barn. "You aren't supposed to eat the bribe."

"I know that *now*."

Ellery smiled and reached for the candy cane she'd tucked into her coat pocket before she'd ventured into the woods.

Ellery patted Sugar's flank as she eased through the narrow gap between the horse and the wall. "Easy, girl. Coming through."

An abrupt silence descended on the barn when she ducked into the empty stall.

Sugar's nostrils quivered in anticipation when she spotted the treat. Without hesitation, the horse plodded into her new home and took the candy cane from Ellery's hand with all the manners of a well-behaved golden retriever.

Ellery patted the velvety nose and made a break for it.

She slid the door slid shut, turned and found herself on the receiving end of three engaging grins.

Sunni Mason had referred to her sons as "boys," so Ellery was taken aback to see grown men in their mid-to-late twenties, not the teenagers she'd expected, standing in front of her. Ink-black hair provided a striking contrast to eyes in various shades of watercolor blue. And in spite of the fact they looked as if they'd been rolling in the straw instead of using it as bedding, all three were tanned and fit and handsome enough to grace the cover of an outdoor magazine.

"I don't know who you are," the tallest one said cheerfully. "But we appreciate the help."

"I rode when I was younger," Ellery admitted, the memory of her parents cheering from the sidelines during her dressage events finding the tender places in her heart. "Peppermint was a treat."

"So are apples." The group's spokesman shot a meaningful look at the guy standing next to him, who looked to be the youngest of Sunni Mason's offspring.

"Sugar obviously has a discerning palate." He grinned back, totally unrepentant. Unlike the other two, who were as clean-cut as Carter, this man's hair brushed the collar of his flannel shirt and a shadow of a beard accentuated his jaw. He was also the only one with the bring-it-on gleam of a daredevil in his eyes.

He glanced at the third man, who'd remained silent during the exchange. "Which one would you prefer? An apple or a candy cane?"

"Oh, no. Don't look at me," he said mildly. "I'm Switzerland, remember?"

While Ellery tried to keep up with their good-natured banter, Sunni poked her head around the door. "How is it going?"

"Piece of cake." Ellery found herself on the receiving end of a mischievous wink. "Or should I say candy?"

"She's a sweetie, all right," Sunni agreed. "That must be why her owner named her Sugar."

"Her disposition?" Switzerland mused. "Or her eating habits?"

Ellery grinned.

"Don't pay any attention to my sons, Ellery. They might be a little overwhelming in triplicate, but I promise they're harmless." The affection in Sunni Mason's voice was in direct contrast to the exasperated look she rolled toward the ceiling. "Now, you boys scrape up the manners I taught you and say hello to Ellery."

"Do we introduce ourselves by birth order or order of importance?" Laughter danced like a flame in the daredevil's cobalt blue eyes.

"Both. Which means you go last." The man who'd spoken to Ellery first stepped forward with a smile. "Brendan Kane. And thanks again for your help."

"She could probably tell it was our first rodeo," his companion said. "I'm Aiden. And the quiet guy holding up the wall over there is Liam."

"Aiden only *thinks* I'm quiet." The man's lips quirked at the corners. "Most of the time I'm ignoring him."

Ellery's knees had turned to liquid. Somehow, she managed to shape her frozen lips into a caricature of a smile as she shook their hands.

Brendan, Liam and Aiden.

Sunni Mason's sons.

And her…brothers.

"I better tell Karen and Isabella the coast is clear," the woman was saying. "That little girl is so excited to meet Sugar, she's been jumping around like a pogo stick the last five minutes."

"I'll tell them." Ellery somehow reached the door without stumbling. Kept her voice from cracking when she told Karen and Bea they could meet Sugar.

Made it back to the inn before the tears started to fall.

* * *

Carter pulled into the gas station and saw a pickup emblazoned with the Castle Falls Outfitters logo hogging two spaces in the parking lot. The empty horse trailer hitched to the back of the truck proof his mom's soft heart had prevailed once again.

He got out of the squad car and plucked the nozzle from the fuel pump just as the Kane brothers spilled out of the station. They spotted the squad car and in what appeared to be a synchronized choreography, changed direction and ambled toward him.

"Officer Friendly." Aiden, river guide turned temporary wrangler, grinned at Carter. "How's it going?"

"That's *Deputy* Friendly to you," Carter drawled. "And everything is great."

One would think that a guy fluent in sarcasm would be able to read the room, but no. If possible, Aiden's grin grew even wider. He hooked his thumbs in the pockets of his faded jeans, leaned a hip against the squad car and made himself comfortable.

"We left your place a little while ago," Liam said. "Sunni was thrilled your mom agreed to give Sugar a home."

"Temporary home," Carter corrected. His eyes narrowed as a thought suddenly occurred to him. "Its name is Sugar? It's a *white* horse?"

"Uh-huh." Brendan cocked his head. "Do you have a problem with white horses? Or horses in general?"

Can I tell you what I wished for, Daddy? I wished for a real live horse that looks just like Snowflake.

Bea had whispered the words when Carter had tucked her into bed after they'd returned home from the parade.

Carter hadn't known what to say. He *never* knew what

to say in the face of a child's absolute certainty that life would unfold exactly the way you thought it should.

Bea would have been ecstatic when the animal arrived. Just like he knew she would be inconsolable when the Kanes loaded Sugar back into the trailer and took her away.

So, no. Carter didn't have a problem with horses. He had a problem with anything that would potentially break his daughter's heart.

"Mom got the call about Sugar and remembered Karen had agreed to host the live nativity this year," Brendan said, not waiting for Carter's answer.

"Which means you have a barn," Liam added. "Sunni decided it was an answerer to prayer."

After all the times Carter had called out to God, he found it a little ironic He'd chosen this particular situation to intervene. But then again, Sunni Mason was the one whose prayers had been answered.

"Your daughter was part of the welcoming committee." Brendan chuckled. "She informed us, very sweetly, of course, that she is no longer a princess. She's a cowgirl."

"And so is one of your guests." Aiden shook his head, open admiration on his face. "We tried for fifteen minutes to coax Sugar into her stall and it took her, what, fifteen seconds?"

"Not even," Liam said.

Carter had never been what some would call a glutton for punishment. Never asked questions he already knew the answer to. But the name slipped out anyway.

"Ellery?"

A knowing look passed from brother to brother.

"What?" Carter demanded.

"Nothing." The lines bracketing Brendan's mouth deepened. "Nothing at all."

Then why did Carter feel like he'd missed the punchline of a joke?

He returned the nozzle to its holder with a little more force than necessary. "I hate to cut this short, but I have to finish entering my reports before shift change."

"Are you coming to the open house at the studio this evening?" Liam asked. "Anna is going to reveal her new design."

Only a guy head over heels in love could make a jewelry demo sound as exciting as watching the Super Bowl.

The envy that spiraled through Carter caught him off guard. He remembered being in Liam's shoes once upon a time, but not everyone was guaranteed a happily-ever-after.

"And Lily has been baking up a storm this week, so I can promise there will be plenty of food," Brendan added, referring to his wife.

"No. Sorry." Carter tried to make it sound sincere. He opened the driver's-side door, hoping they would take the hint. "My mom and Bea will most likely be there, though. She texted me a few hours ago and asked if I'd keep an eye on the desk this evening."

"What about Ellery?" Aiden asked. "Will she be there?"

Carter's back teeth snapped together. "I have no idea what her plans are. She's a *guest*."

Brendan tipped his head back and studied the clouds as if he'd never seen them before. And Aiden, the guy who always had a snappy comeback, didn't say anything at all.

A little suspicious. And completely out of character.

Too bad Carter couldn't arrest them for disturbing his peace.

"We'll all be taking a shift in the barn over the next few days," Brendan said. "I'm sure we'll see you around."

"Thanks for the warning."

They laughed as if Carter had cracked a joke and sauntered back to their truck. Halfway across the parking lot, Liam turned around.

"Ah… Carter?"

Carter sensed an apology coming. He'd discovered that Liam was the least likely of the three brothers to be a pain in the neck.

"Yeah?"

"Anna would kill me if I didn't remind you that you're welcome to bring a plus-one to our wedding."

"A plus-one?"

"You know…an extra *guest*." Liam looked like he was wrestling down a smile.

Okay, so he'd been wrong. Liam could be a pain in the neck. He wasn't very subtle, either, because it was obvious he was referring to Ellery.

"I might be working on Christmas Eve." Carter didn't know his schedule yet but there was one thing he was sure of.

Ellery would be long gone by then.

Chapter Ten

"Are you sure you don't want to come with us, Ellery?" Karen bent over and zipped up Bea's coat. "Anna Leighton creates beautiful jewelry, and we won't be gone more than an hour or so."

"I'm going to make a bracelet!" Bea chimed in.

"It sounds like fun, but I'm looking forward to curling up by the fire tonight. Reading a good book."

Continuing to recover from the emotional ambush that had taken place that afternoon.

The tears that had been simmering in Ellery's eyes threatened to overflow again. She blinked them away before Karen noticed.

Ellery had allowed herself to daydream about her first meeting with her brothers, even practiced what she would say, but the reality of seeing them face-to-face had brought a flood of emotions she couldn't even put a name to.

"I can make you a bracelet, too," Bea offered.

Hold. It. Together. "That's very thoughtful of you, sweetie."

"If you need anything, let Carter know." Karen looped her purse over her shoulder. "He's holding down the fort until we get home."

Carter was the last person Ellery wanted to see simply because the man saw too much. But she nodded and held her smile in place until they left.

The door closed, sealing off Bea's excited chatter, and silence descended on the lobby. Suddenly, in spite of what Ellery had told Karen, the thought of retreating to her room for the remainder of the evening held no appeal. She'd already spent the last few hours staring into the fire, reliving the moment she'd met her brothers.

Restlessness overrode Ellery's desire for privacy and pushed her toward the door. Giving in to an impulse she couldn't explain, she grabbed a coat from the hook and stepped outside.

Maybe Sugar was feeling as out of place and confused as she was tonight.

The cold stung Ellery's cheeks as she walked toward the barn. A light glowing in the peak of the roof guided her steps down the footpath. She opened the door and slipped inside, fumbled with the switch on the wall. A burst of light chased the shadows into the corners.

Slow-motion images began to unfold in Ellery's mind as she made her way to Sugar's stall.

Her brothers had faces now. Distinct personalities. Physically, they resembled each other but it had only taken Ellery a few moments to realize their personalities were as unique as snowflakes. Brendan had a firstborn's natural confidence. Liam, the quiet, steady strength of a peacemaker.

But Aiden…

Seeing him had been the biggest shock of all. Aiden looked to be no more than a year or two older than Ellery.

Her stomach folded in on itself again.

It hadn't escaped Ellery's notice that her brothers seemed comfortable with each other and their place in the family. And the way they'd teased each other…it spoke of a bond tested by time.

Had they grown up together? Was she the only one who'd been adopted by a different family?

And if the answer to that last question was yes, then *why*?

Ellery didn't understand why her parents had been so secretive about her background. They hadn't even told Jameson, a close family friend, the details surrounding her birth.

Sugar backed into the corner of the stall when Ellery unlatched the door.

"Hey, girl. Just thought I'd see how you were doing."

Sugar's nostrils flared but she didn't move.

Ellery hadn't had an opportunity to study the animal until now, but what she saw had her reaching for the bucket of grooming tools on the floor. Armed with a currycomb and a pocketful of treats, Ellery opened the door and joined Sugar in the stall.

The horse's ears flattened as Ellery reached out to stroke the tangled mane.

"Easy," she soothed. "No one's going to hurt you. This is a safe place."

A ribbon of wind unfurled between the stalls, lifting up stray bits of hay and twirling them in the air like confetti.

Ellery's head snapped up and she saw Carter silhouetted in the doorway.

Okay. Maybe not so safe.

Carter had been raiding the fridge when he noticed a light in the barn. His mom and Bea were attending the open house at Anna's studio, the overnight guests had made dinner reservations at a local supper club and the only car parked outside the inn was a cherry-red Lexus.

So, through the process of elimination, it left only one person with a penchant for trespassing.

He'd put the cranberry bread pudding away and retrieved his coat from the entryway.

The cold air seared Carter's lungs, and a full moon cast silver-blue shadows on the snow as he walked across the yard.

He wasn't sure what Ellery would be doing out there this late at night, but he sure didn't expect to find her standing inside one of the stalls, patiently working a metal comb through the tangle of burrs in the horse's mane.

The expression on her face told Carter she hadn't expected to see him, either.

"What are you doing here?"

Funny. Carter had been about to ask her the same thing.

"I saw a light...and even though Bea assures me that Sugar is the smartest horse in the world, I had my doubts she knew how to work a wall switch."

Carter hadn't realized how much he wanted to see Ellery smile until he failed at the task.

"I thought she might be lonely."

"Lonely."

"She's in a strange place. Doesn't know anyone." Ellery turned back her work, her face veiled in shadows.

Why did Carter get the feeling she wasn't talking about the horse?

"The inn isn't a working dude ranch," he reminded her. "Sunni Mason promised to send volunteers to help out with stuff like this."

"I know. They're not here tonight, though," Ellery said simply. She paused, murmuring an encouragement when the comb snagged in another knot, and fed the horse a small treat.

Maybe that was the secret to getting Bea to stand still when he brushed her hair.

His gaze shifted back to Ellery. She'd draped her leather jacket over a bale of hay, revealing a thin green sweater that coaxed out a hint of jade in her aquamarine eyes. Jeans with fancy embroidery decorating the pockets were tucked into the pair of boots Carter remembered her wearing the night they'd met.

"Did you plan to go outside at all while you were here?"

Ellery glanced down. Batted at a piece of straw clinging to the hem of her sweater. "What do you mean?"

"Most of the guests who stay at the inn in December are part of the cross-country ski or snowshoe set. They come prepared for the weather."

"I came here for a change of scenery, remember?"

Oh, Carter remembered what she'd claimed. But he couldn't imagine that included a drafty barn.

Another gust of wind rattled the window casing and spooked Sugar. Ellery didn't even flinch as the fifteen-hundred-pound animal performed an impromptu hip-hop dance inside the stall. She didn't dive for cover, either. She moved *closer*, murmuring something under her breath that Carter couldn't hear. Whatever it was, Sugar immediately settled down.

"Should I add horse whisperer to Mom's food-critic-or-reporter-for-a-magazine theory?" Carter asked. "Because according to Aiden and his brothers, you're a bona fide cowgirl. I wouldn't be surprised if they recruited you for barn chores this week."

"They…they're coming back?"

"All of the Kanes are involved with the shelter in some way or another. And Aiden got the all-clear from his doctor to resume his normal activities, so I'm guessing he'll be here, too."

"Doctor?" Ellery was staring at him now. "Was he... sick?"

"No." Carter made himself useful and peeled off a flake of hay. Stuffed it into the net hanging on the wall. "Aiden was in an accident a few months ago."

Ellery's arm dropped to her side. He had her full attention now. "Karen mentioned that he's a guide. Did it happen when he was out on the river?"

"No." Carter hesitated. Normally, he didn't talk about the job, but in this particular case, the investigation was closed and the details common knowledge, thanks to the efficiency of the small-town grapevine. "It was a hit-and-run."

The color ebbed from Ellery's cheeks, and Carter was taken aback by her strong reaction.

Ellery had all but admitted her visit to Castle Falls had been based on a whim. A sign she was as capricious as Jennifer. But his ex-wife wouldn't have worried about a horse being lonely. Or been moved by the plight of a total stranger.

"Aiden bounced back faster than people thought he would." The image of Aiden's truck, upside down at the base of a massive white pine, had become etched in Carter's mind. "Bruised ribs, a broken arm. Messed up his knee pretty badly, too. When I arrived at the scene and saw the damage, I couldn't believe he'd survived."

Ellery knelt down and began to inspect the horse's hooves. A shadow fell across her face, hiding her expression. "Did you find the person responsible?"

"It was the younger brother of one of the teenagers Aiden had been mentoring." Carter shook his head. "They're both working at Castle Falls Outfitters on the weekends."

"The boy was ordered to pay restitution?"

"Aiden calls it *restoration*. And it was his idea."

"You don't think people can change?"

"I haven't seen a lot of evidence, no." And his ex-wife certainly hadn't given Carter the opportunity. "I don't agree with Aiden, but considering his past, I guess I shouldn't be surprised he gave the kid a second chance."

"Why not?"

"Because he got one."

Ellery was careful not to let Carter see her reaction.

A second chance?

What did that mean? Because Aiden had survived the accident? Or was Carter referring to something else?

She rose to her feet again, trying to sort through all the information he'd unwittingly provided.

"Wh-when did you say it happened?"

"September."

Almost two months before her brothers had reached out to the adoption agency.

"And you were there?"

Carter nodded. "I arrived at the scene when the paramedics were getting him ready for transport to the hospital."

"It must be difficult…to be one of the first people at the scene when something bad happens."

"With the job, you can't let your emotions take over. You have to rely on your training," Carter said. But the shadow that chased through his eyes told Ellery it didn't come without a cost.

"Still…to find out the person who got hurt was someone you know…" Ellery struggled to keep her voice steady. "You're close in age. You must have gone to school with Aiden and his brothers?"

"We didn't grow up together, if that's what you mean.

Mom bought the Evergreen the summer between my freshman and sophomore year in high school. She'd worked in restaurants to support us after my dad left, but it was always her dream to own an inn.

"The Kanes were transplants, too. There were a lot of rumors flying around when they came to town. Everyone at school thought they were bad news and, from what I recall, they didn't exactly do anything to change people's opinion."

"Transplants?" Ellery's pulse spiked. "From where?"

"Detroit, I think." Carter shrugged. "I had a few classes with Liam, but they pretty much kept to themselves. I spent my free time helping Mom get ready to open and enlisted right after graduation, so in a way, I was an outsider, too."

A dozen questions popped up in Ellery's mind, but at the moment, her focus was on the man who grabbed an extra brush from the bucket and began to attack the mat of burrs on the tail of the horse he didn't want taking up space in his barn.

"How long were you in the Navy?"

"I served two tours—and then I accepted a job with the sheriff's department. It's a good fit."

Short and matter-of-fact. But Ellery read between the lines. Somewhere in that time frame, Carter had married. Had a child.

Put his trust in his training instead of his emotions.
And God.

"You like Castle Falls?" Ellery ventured.

"I always wanted to come back."

"It is a beautiful area," she said softly.

"True." Bitterness seeped into Carter's voice. "Although most of the people who come here aren't interested in making it their permanent home."

Had Carter's ex-wife fallen into that category? Or were there other reasons she'd left?

"My... The Kanes did."

"Castle Falls Outfitters is a family business," Carter said. "Rich, Sunni's husband, passed away not long after they came here. Brendan took over the business when he was about sixteen but all three of them have poured their heart and soul into making it a success ever since."

So. She'd guessed right. Her brothers had spent their formative years together before they'd moved to Castle Falls. But what had their lives been like before that?

Ellery's earliest memories were playing in the yard of her family's sprawling estate outside of Grand Rapids.

"When I met them today... I could tell they're close," she murmured.

"And extremely devoted to Sunni, which explains why they can't say no to her schemes." Carter aimed a pointed look at the horse.

"Sugar is not a scheme," Ellery protested. "She needed a home until Christmas and you had an empty barn. A perfect match."

"It might be a great solution for Sunni Mason, but she isn't the one who has to comfort a heartbroken five-year-old when it's time to say goodbye."

Ellery felt a tug on her heart.

Based on what Karen had told her, Carter had already done that once and it must have torn him apart.

Lord, give me the right words to say.

From the time she was a child, Ellery had accompanied her parents on short-term medical mission trips. If they'd shielded her from the poverty and sickness, Ellery would have missed out on the joy that bloomed in the midst of it, too.

And although losing them had left a huge void in Ellery's life, she knew they wouldn't have wanted her to close off her heart to avoid any more pain.

"Bea will be sad," Ellery said carefully. "And I know you want to protect her...but I think that caring about something, being thankful for what it brought to our lives, whether it's for a moment or a month or a lifetime, makes our hearts *bigger*.

"You don't want to take that away from her, Carter. You don't want Bea to be afraid to...love."

Carter went completely still and the disbelief in his eyes made Ellery regret her impulsive words. She'd already been accused of trespassing...now it appeared that she'd crossed a boundary and encroached on his personal life, too.

The cell phone clipped on Carter's hip began to ring—*thank You, Lord*—and Sugar performed that little side shuffle again. With a muttered apology, he stepped outside the stall to answer it.

"It's okay," Ellery whispered, stroking the horse's nose to settle her down. Sugar quieted immediately, but Ellery's heart continued to beat in double time.

Several seconds of silence ticked by before she heard a clipped "On my way."

Carter appeared in the doorway again. His expression hadn't changed but the intensity of his gaze, the set of his jaw, told Ellery that something terrible had happened.

His next words confirmed her suspicions. "That was dispatch. Domestic disturbance." Carter was already moving toward the door. "Mom and Bea are on their way back, so you don't have to worry about the desk being unattended."

Ellery wasn't worried about the inn. She was worried about *him*.

Every time Carter saw the dark side of life, it formed

another layer around his heart, making it more difficult for the light to get in.

"Carter." Without thinking, Ellery reached out and caught his hand. "Be careful."

Carter froze, and Ellery waited for him to say something cynical.

Carter's fingers tightened around hers. So quickly, Ellery wondered if she'd imagined it.

And then he was gone.

Chapter Eleven

Ellery collapsed on the nearest hay bale.

If the fleeting touch of Carter's hand was all it took to make her knees weak, it would be wise to take her own advice.

The feelings she was developing for Carter weren't the only thing she found confusing. What he'd shared about her brothers was confusing, too. And troubling.

Ellery returned to the house and climbed the stairs to the second floor.

As tempting as it was to make herself a cup of tea, Carter's mother was as intuitive as her son. It would be safer to retire to her room before Karen and Bea got home.

Her phone chirped on the nightstand, letting her know a new text had arrived.

She picked it up and for the second time that day, felt the world slide off its axis.

It was a screenshot from a newspaper. "Darren Kane Sentenced to Twenty Years in Prison."

Below the headline were the words Call me.

The number belonged to Dwayne Howard.

Ellery dialed Jameson's instead.

He picked up on the first ring. "Ellery—"

"I just got a message from Dwayne Howard." Ellery struggled to keep her voice steady. "I thought you agreed we weren't going to hire a private investigator."

"I put Dwayne on retainer just in case we needed him." the attorney admitted. "I had no idea he would go ahead and do some digging on his own. He told me about the article this morning but I had no idea he planned to forward it to you."

"Darren Kane." The name tasted foreign on her tongue. "Is he...my biological father?"

"Based on what Dwayne discovered, it appears that way."

The lump in Ellery's throat doubled in size. "What did he do?"

"Fraud. Kane was a long-distance truck driver who decided it would be more lucrative to switch to construction. And it was. The pseudo-company he started bilked senior citizens out of their retirement savings until law enforcement caught up to him. Based on the information Howard uncovered, Darren Kane was a master manipulator. Someone who recognized when people were vulnerable and exploited it for his own gain."

A trait Jameson obviously feared the man had passed on to her siblings.

Images of Aiden's mischievous wink and Liam's wry smile flashed in Ellery's mind.

"My brothers aren't in prison." She instinctively came to their defense. "They own their own business. They're involved in the community."

"It doesn't mean the Kanes don't have an agenda where you're concerned," Jameson said. "I'm still not convinced the letter they sent wasn't a fishing expedition."

Ellery's stomach churned. Her heart wanted to reject Jameson's concerns, but the seeds of doubt had already been sown during her conversation with Carter.

They're committed to making the family business a success. They're a tight group.

What if Aiden's stay in the hospital and the physical therapy afterward had drained the family's savings? Put their livelihood at risk?

Maybe Jameson was right. Maybe they didn't need a sister as much as they needed what that sister could provide.

Maybe she was a means to an end.

And even though Ellery had meant what she'd said to Carter about not being afraid to love, her heart, Ellery realized, wasn't quite ready for another loss.

"You accomplished your goal. Now it's time to let Dwayne take over." Jameson's voice broke into her thoughts. "Please come home."

Ellery closed her eyes. "All right."

"Tomorrow?"

"Tomorrow."

Jameson's sigh of relief rattled in her ear. "Let me know when you're back in town. Trust me, Elle. A little distance between you and Castle Falls is what you need right now."

Then why did it feel like her heart was being torn apart?

Ellery ended the call and dropped into the chair by the window. Drew her knees against her chest and watched the moon struggling to free itself from the branches of the trees.

Closed her eyes and tried to pray but the words got tangled up in her emotions...

She woke with a start when someone touched her arm.

Ellery blinked, trying to make sense of the changes around her. The fire had died out and the moon was gone, cloaking the room in darkness.

"Miss El'ry?"

The tears that clogged Bea's voice brought Ellery to her

feet. Her muscles, cramped from having fallen asleep in the chair, screamed in protest.

"Bea? What's the matter, sweetheart? Did you have a bad dream?"

Bea shook her head.

"There's something wrong with Gramma."

The sun was rising when Carter got off duty. Which was a good thing, because he could barely see straight. The adrenaline that had kept the synapses firing in his brain throughout the night was wearing off and exhaustion seeped in to take its place.

A light glowed in the kitchen window, forcing him to make a decision. Coffee or a few more hours of sleep?

He opted for coffee.

Praise music filtered from the kitchen, a welcome relief from the piercing shriek of multiple sirens still playing in the background of Carter's head.

He pushed open the door and saw Bea perched on a stool at the butcher-block island, ten pink toes peeking out from the hem of her favorite nightgown.

No matter what had happened during Carter's shift, seeing his daughter warmed his heart like an early spring thaw.

"And here the weatherman said the sun wasn't going to shine today," he teased.

Bea's head lifted at the sound of his voice.

And then she promptly burst into tears.

"Hey." Carter crossed the room in two strides and scooped her into his arms. "What's the matter?"

The question only caused the sobs to increase in volume.

The door between the dining room and kitchen swung open and Ellery charged in.

"Bea…" She stopped short at the sight of him. "You're home."

Worry and weariness lurked behind the relief Carter saw in Ellery's eyes. And even though she cobbled together a smile, Carter was struck by an overwhelming urge to wrap his arms around her, too.

"Would someone like to tell me what's going on?" The storm inside of his daughter had subsided a bit, but Carter continued to pat Bea's back, absorbing the shudders that rocked her tiny frame.

Ellery's gaze rested on Bea for a moment. Her hesitation was a sign she was choosing her words with their audience in mind. "Karen isn't feeling well this morning, so Bea and I are making breakfast for the guests."

Judging from Bea's reaction, Carter knew there was more to the story, but now wasn't the time to push for details.

"I made a cup of ginger tea for Karen," Ellery continued calmly. "Would you mind taking it to her while Bea and I start the waffles?"

"Only if you promise to save some for me." Carter tickled Bea's ribs before he set her down on the stool again and was rewarded with a throaty giggle.

"I can't eat them all, Daddy."

Carter picked up the tray Ellery had prepared. Coffee and a few hours of sleep would have to wait.

He knocked on his mother's door before letting himself inside. The shades were drawn, bathing the room in shadows. Karen stirred when Carter set the tray down on the nightstand.

"Carter?" She struggled to sit up. "What time is it? I haven't started the coffee…" With a low groan, she collapsed against the pillows again. "Or breakfast. The guests—"

"Don't worry about breakfast or the guests." Carter squeezed her hand. Just as he suspected, it felt hot to the touch. "Everything is taken care of."

"Bea—"

"She's fine, too. In the kitchen with Ellery making breakfast."

"I don't know what I would have done without her." Karen ran a shaky hand through her hair and for the first time, Carter noticed the bruise on her temple.

"Did you fall?" Worry spiked all over again. "The only thing Ellery said was that you weren't feeling well."

Karen managed a wan smile. "It was a combination of both, I'm afraid. I had a headache when I went to bed and it got worse, so I decided to take something for it. On the way down the hall, I started to feel light-headed. The next thing I knew, Bea was standing over me. She must have heard me fall and woke up.

"I could tell she was terrified. I tried to tell her that I would be okay, but she ran away. I didn't realize she'd gone to get Ellery." Karen's eyelids fluttered, as if the effort to keep them open drained her energy. "Ellery calmed Bea down and helped me get back into bed. I convinced her that all I needed was an ice pack and a few hours of sleep and I'd pop out of bed this morning, as good as new."

She didn't look as good as new.

Carter pressed his fingers against her wrist. "What's your pain on a scale of one to ten?"

"Three…"

"Squared?" Carter knew his mother too well. "I think you caught the virus that's been going around."

"I don't have time for a virus," Karen moaned. "I've got rooms to clean after the guests check out this morning and Maddie asked if I would provide the refreshments for the Christmas tea at the library's open house tomorrow…"

"I can pick something up at the grocery store."

Based on the way his mom flinched, Carter's offer hadn't put her mind at ease.

"It's a *Victorian* tea," she said. "There's a special menu. Cucumber sandwiches. Scones…clotted cream."

Clotted cream?

Carter scrubbed his hand across his chin. Okay, if it wasn't carrot sticks or cheese and crackers, they did have a problem.

"Under the circumstances, I'm sure Maddie will understand if you have to cancel—"

"Or Carter and I can divide and conquer."

Carter hadn't heard Ellery come into the room.

She walked over to the bed and smiled down at Karen. "Don't worry about a thing. All you have to do today is concentrate on getting better."

If Karen would have had more energy, she would have protested. Or maybe not. Because the frown between her brows eased and she closed her eyes again.

Carter followed Ellery into the hallway and pulled the door shut with a gentle click.

"Divide and conquer?" he echoed.

"You take the upstairs and I'll take the kitchen."

"Why?"

"Because I spent a summer in London, and clotted cream is a little above your pay grade."

The statement should have reminded Carter that Ellery lived in a different world. Instead, he battled an irresistible urge to smile.

"What I meant was, why did you offer to help?"

Ellery appeared genuinely shocked by the question.

"Because your mom needs us."

Us.

It sounded…good.

Too good.

Which was really, really bad.

Chapter Twelve

Later that evening, Ellery finished washing the last of the dishes and hung the damp towel on the rack.

The refrigerator held four dozen miniature fruit tarts, the filling for the sandwiches and a crock filled with clotted cream. Tidy rows of scones cooled on wire racks.

She'd brought a sampling of the menu to Karen's room, but in spite of the woman's claim that she "felt a little better," Ellery couldn't see any signs of improvement.

She'd managed to coax Karen into taking a few sips of tea, but the crackers on the nightstand had gone untouched. Karen's cheeks were flushed with color, a sign the fever hadn't gone away. Neither had the pain from the headache that accompanied the virus, no matter how hard she tried to downplay her symptoms.

There was no way Ellery could walk out on a woman who'd been nothing but kind since the day she'd arrived in Castle Falls.

And Carter...

Ellery hadn't been able to walk out on him, either.

She'd sent Jameson a quick text explaining that she'd had to delay her return for a day, but now the day was over.

It was time to find Carter and let him know she'd be leaving first thing in the morning.

There was no sign of him in the lobby or the gathering room, but Ellery could hear the faint strains of Christmas music coming from a room that hadn't been included in Carter's tour of the inn. She guessed they'd carved out some space for a private retreat. A place the family could relax and enjoy some time together, undisturbed.

Ellery veered down a narrow hall that branched off from the back entryway. Tapped on the door.

No answer.

Cautiously, she turned the knob and nudged it open. Peeked into a spacious living room that lived up to its name.

The logs burning in the fireplace cast a golden glow over the books scattered on the rug and the toys overflowing from a wooden chest in the corner.

And the man stretched out on the sofa.

Ellery's breath tangled in her lungs.

Carter lay on his side, one arm pillowed underneath his head, the other resting on his abdomen. Ellery could see the gentle rise and fall of his chest. The fringe of dark lashes that fanned out on his cheekbones.

In uniform, it was easy to see the warrior in Carter. The Navy SEAL who'd transitioned to full-time deputy. But now, relaxed in sleep, Carter looked younger. Vulnerable.

And the feelings Carter stirred made Ellery feel vulnerable, too.

She backed out of the room, careful not to disturb him, and padded back up the stairs. Hesitated for a moment on the landing before turning left, toward the family suite.

She'd broken so many rules already, what was one more?

Ellery found Bea standing on a stool in front of the bathroom sink, humming while she dragged a brush through her hair.

Affection bubbled up inside of Ellery.

The little girl had been a trouper all day. Ellery had kept Bea busy in the kitchen all afternoon so that Karen could rest. She'd let her mix the crust for the fruit tarts and layer paper-thin slices of cucumbers between slices of bread while Carter prepared for the next wave of guests.

No wonder he was exhausted. He'd worked twenty-four hours straight without complaint.

"Where's Daddy?" Bea's face crumpled when she spotted Ellery in the doorway. "Is he sick, too?"

"No, sweetheart, your Daddy is fine," Ellery hastened to reassure her. "I'm sure he'll be here in a few minutes to tuck you in. Would you like me to read you a bedtime story while you wait?"

"Uh-huh." Without hesitation, Bea hopped off the stool and strung her arms around Ellery's waist. "I'm glad you're here, Miss El'ry."

Ellery returned the hug. "So am I," she murmured.

Oh, leaving was going to be so much more difficult than Ellery had first thought. In the space of a few short days, Bea had worked her way into Ellery's heart.

But as Jameson was so quick to remind her, she didn't belong in Castle Falls. And Bea didn't belong to her, either.

That didn't stop Ellery from holding tight to the little girl's hand, though, as Bea led her down the hall. Bea's bedroom was a wonderland of pink-and-white gingham. Dress-up clothes spilled over the side of an antique steamer trunk. A porcelain tea set similar to Karen's formed the centerpiece for a tiny wooden table and matching chairs.

Bea burrowed under the patchwork quilt, careful not to displace the herd of stuffed ponies lined up at the foot of her bed.

Ellery sat down on the edge of the mattress and looked

at the stack of books on the nightstand. "Do you have a favorite?"

Bea chose one from the top of the stack and snuggled closer. It was a children's version of the nativity story and Bea giggled as Ellery tried to imitate a cast of secondary characters that included a sheep, a donkey and a cross-eyed camel.

Ellery was about to reach for another, but Bea bent down and picked up a colorful backpack next to the bed, her smile almost shy.

"Do you want to see the one I wrote?"

Ellery was intrigued. "You wrote a book?"

"Uh-huh. Miss Maddie read a story called *The Best Christmas Ever* and then she gave all of us paper to make one, too. I didn't know how to spell all the words, so I drew the pictures and Miss Maddie helped with the letters."

Bea reached into the backpack and pulled out a "book" made from pieces of construction paper stapled together. The cover alone drew a smile. A little girl with yellow pigtails and big blue eyes stood beside a Christmas tree strikingly similar to the one in the Bristow's family room.

"Isabella's Best Christmas Ever." Ellery read the title aloud.

"Miss Maddie said I should practice writing my *whole* name," Bea confided, settling under the covers once more.

With every turn of the page, Ellery was given a precious glimpse into Bea's heart.

Decorating Christmas cookies. Ice-skating on the pond. Building a snow fort. A pony of her own...

Ellery's heart stuttered when she saw a dark-haired man dressed in brown from head to toe, a shiny gold star over his heart.

Written in neat block letters underneath the picture were three words.

Daddy smiles more.

Ellery's heart ached for the little girl. And for Carter. Didn't he realize that he kept a shield around his emotions even when he wasn't on duty? One that kept the people who loved him at arm's length?

"Do you like it?" Bea sounded a little uncertain. "There's extra pages 'cause Gramma came to get me and I didn't have time to finish it…"

"It's perfect," Ellery quickly assured her.

"Prayers next." Bea's smile had returned and she bowed her head. "God…it's Bea. Thank You for Gramma and Daddy and Sugar and Miss El'ry. And help Gramma feel better so we can have ice cream tomorrow." One blue eye opened a crack. "It's your turn."

"God…" Ellery didn't know quite where to start. Her prayers had been as raw as her emotions lately, pouring out from her heart in fits and stops. Her mom had always told her that it was impossible to get weighed down by circumstances when your hands were lifted in praise, so she followed Bea's example and listed some of the things she was thankful for.

God's goodness. His love and faithfulness.

All things Ellery had experienced in the past that shouldn't have left any room for worry about the future.

Bea echoed Ellery's whispered "amen" and it turned into a yawn.

"Is Daddy coming soon? My eyes are…" Another yawn. "Falling asleep."

"He's here." Carter stood in the doorway. A little rumpled, but upright and in control once again.

And way too attractive for Ellery's peace of mind.

This was the second time today that Ellery had come to Carter's rescue.

A dad was never off duty, but he must have fallen asleep

on the job. Because the last thing Carter remembered was sending Bea upstairs to brush her teeth and get ready for bed.

He padded into the room. "What did I miss?"

"Stories and prayers," Bea sang out. "But not good-night kisses."

Carter couldn't prevent his gaze from dropping to Ellery's lips any more than he could have stopped his heart midbeat.

A hint of rose bloomed in her cheeks as she vaulted off the bed.

"I… Good night." Ellery smiled at Bea and slipped past him without a backward glance.

There were things Carter wanted to say. *Thank you* being at the top of the list. But he didn't dare follow her.

Not with good-night kisses on his mind.

Carter tucked the blankets around Bea's shoulders. "Sleep tight, Izzybea."

"Is Gramma going to pick me up after school tomorrow?"

"I'm not sure."

Karen's room had been Carter's first stop on his way down the hall and her "I'm feeling better" would have been more believable if she hadn't been shivering underneath the down comforter.

Whatever had grabbed hold of Karen didn't seem in any hurry to let go.

"But she promised we could go to The Happy Cow for ice cream afterward." Bea's lower lip trembled. "It's a special flavor and everything."

Carter vaguely remembered the ice cream parlor being on the list of businesses that participated in the Countdown to Christmas every year.

"Well, we can't pass up a special flavor, now can we?" Carter said. "If Gramma can't take you, we'll figure something out."

Even though he was on the schedule for the rest of the week.

And had an inn to run.

Bea sank back into the pillow, the absolute trust on her face a gift Carter knew he didn't deserve. He pressed a kiss to her forehead and turned out the lamp.

Now he could finally get that cup of coffee.

The kitchen looked spotless, everything in its proper place. Carter expected to find two inches of liquid mulch in the bottom of the carafe, but Ellery had brewed a fresh pot. He filled his mug and scanned the oversize calendar on the wall.

Every square was filled.

Carter shouldn't have been surprised. His mom took on way more than she should…especially this time of year.

Refreshments for the library's Victorian tea for instance.

Carter opened the fridge and saw the fruit of Ellery's labor in the form of dozens of mouthwatering tarts. The sandwiches were the size of his index finger, but the clotted cream actually looked like something he'd like to eat.

He snagged one of the scones and took a bite. Heard a discreet cough behind him.

Carter glanced over his shoulder.

Busted.

Ellery stood in the threshold between the dining room and kitchen, arms folded across her chest. But in an oversize fuzzy sweater the color of a ripe peach and loose-fitting lounge pants, she looked about as threatening as one of Bea's stuffed ponies.

One perfectly shaped sable brow lifted. "Isn't stealing a crime?"

"Only if there's evidence that one was committed." Carter popped the rest of the scone into his mouth. "Do you want one?"

"Resorting to bribery, Deputy Bristow?" The stern look Ellery leveled in his direction belied the teasing smile that danced at the corners of her lips. "I'm shocked."

And Carter was still shocked at how easily Ellery's smiles could slip through his defenses.

"Thanks for helping out today," Carter said. "We don't usually put the guests to work."

Because that was what Ellery was. A *guest*. Something Carter was having to remind himself of on a regular basis lately.

"I enjoy spending time in the kitchen," Ellery murmured. "It's relaxing."

"Most people prefer to relax by the fire."

"I'm not most people."

Carter was beginning to realize that. He also realized that Ellery hadn't moved from the doorway. Her posture had changed, too. Hands fisted at her sides now, shoulders tense. Ellery hadn't returned to the kitchen for a snack. She'd sought him out for a reason.

"Did you need something?"

"No…" Ellery's teeth nipped her lower lip. "How is Karen doing?"

"If you ask her, she's fine," Carter said. "But I decided a second opinion was in order and called the after-hours line at the clinic. Dr. Wallis wants to see her first thing in the morning."

As dangerous as Ellery's smiles were, Carter preferred them to the frown that knit her forehead.

"Don't worry, though. I'll make breakfast before we leave." He walked over to the wall and with a swipe of his finger, erased strawberry crepes from the menu.

Flashed a smile.

"I hope you like cereal."

Chapter Thirteen

The inn disappeared in Ellery's rearview mirror as she turned onto the county road at the end of the driveway.

Her phone was charging, moisture beaded on the lid of the travel mug riding in the console…and the back seat of her Lexus was packed with refreshments for a Victorian tea.

Because Ellery hadn't been able to tell Carter she was checking out in the morning after all.

She'd packed her suitcase and made her way down to the kitchen, only to discover that Karen wasn't improving… and that she was totally susceptible to handsome men who brazened it out when they were caught foraging for food.

And teased her with a smile when they changed the breakfast menu.

Now if only Ellery could convince Jameson she'd made the right decision by delaying her departure. Again.

But what were the chances she would run into her brothers at the local library? They didn't exactly look like the kind of men who would attend a Victorian tea.

Ellery drove past the city limits sign and parked in front of the two-story brick building she'd noticed during the sleigh ride. After retrieving the plastic containers from the back seat, she made her way up the snow-dusted sidewalk.

The wide double oak doors looked as if they'd been hewn from the trees when the town had been founded, but when Ellery stepped inside, she was astonished to see that the interior of the library looked like a cross between a comfortable living room and a coffee shop.

"Good morning!" The woman behind the circulation desk spotted her. "Can I help you?"

"Maddie Montgomery?" Ellery guessed.

"Nope! Connie Donohue, assistant librarian and loyal sidekick. Sometimes comic relief." She pointed to the narrow corridor between two walls of books. "Maddie and some of the volunteers are setting up for the tea. Go through biographies and poetry, take a left at Shakespeare and follow the historical romances until you see the conference room."

Ellery chuckled. "Thanks."

She followed the woman's creative directions to the conference room and peeked inside. Two women, one a statuesque blonde, the other a slender redhead, seemed to be taking instructions from the petite, bespectacled young woman wearing a vintage gown made from tiers of champagne-colored lace.

Three heads turned in Ellery's direction when she stepped into the room.

"Maddie?" Ellery looked at the woman in lace. Her companions had dressed up for the event, too, but their dresses were more modern in style. It made sense the librarian would wear an outfit that reflected the theme of the event.

"Yes!" Maddie Montgomery glided toward Ellery, her leather ballet flats barely making a sound against the hardwood floor. "Oh, this looks amazing. And heavy!"

Laughing, she motioned to a linen-covered table near the fireplace. "We left a spot for the food right over there."

Ellery set the trays next to a centerpiece made up of crimson poinsettias, sprigs of holly and white roses. Turning, she found herself on the receiving end of not one, but three openly curious smiles.

Because they hadn't been expecting a total stranger to drop off the refreshments.

Ellery smiled back. "I'm—"

"Ellery Marshall." Maddie didn't wait for her to finish the introduction. "You're staying at the Evergreen."

"Ah…yes." What Ellery had heard about small-town grapevines must be true. Although where the information had originated, she had no idea.

"Thank you for bringing the refreshments," the blonde volunteer chimed in. "When word got out that Karen was providing the food, registrations started pouring in. People have been trying to coax her to open a catering business on the side for years."

Confession time.

"Actually…" Ellery released the breath she hadn't realized she'd been holding. "Karen wasn't feeling well this weekend and she gave me permission to take over the kitchen."

Maddie's fern-green eyes rounded. "You made all this?"

"Yes." Ellery glanced down at the tray. She'd followed Karen's menu and added a few touches of her own. "I hope you don't mind."

"Mind?" The woman with the chestnut hair echoed. "Everything looks absolutely delicious! Are you a chef, too?"

"No." Bittersweet memories of working beside her mom in the kitchen misted Ellery's eyes. "I…do a little of this and a little of that."

"Well, you certainly do it well." The blonde chuckled. "Brendan described you as 'very capable.' And believe me, coming from him that's high praise."

Ellery's heart lurched against her rib cage. "Brendan?"

"I'm sorry. Where are my manners?" Laughter sparkled in the violet-blue eyes. "I'm Lily Kane. Brendan is my husband. One of the guys who tried to play cowboy at the Evergreen when they transferred Sugar to her new home."

Lily Kane.

Ellery struggled to keep her smile in place. It hadn't occurred to her that her brothers might be married. Have families of their own.

"It's nice to meet you," she murmured.

"And this is Anna Leighton." Lily introduced the woman with the chestnut hair. "Anna is a *future* Mrs. Kane," she added cheerfully. "Although technically, I suppose we could say the same thing about Maddie."

"It's only fair that Aiden and I wait our turn," the librarian demurred. "Liam and Anna got engaged first."

Ellery tried to process what she'd just heard.

Lily, married to Brendan. Maddie Montgomery and Anna Leighton, her brothers'…fiancées?

"Congratulations." Ellery practically gasped the word. "To both of you. When…when are the weddings taking place?"

"Anna and Liam are getting married on Christmas Eve." Lily exchanged a quick glance with her future sisters-in-law and, for some inexplicable reason, everyone's smiles dimmed for a moment.

Maddie was the first to recover.

"And it's going to be beautiful," she said. "Just like the bride."

Anna linked arms with Maddie and Lily. "And bridesmaids."

The three shared a smile.

Ellery swallowed hard. These women weren't a group of volunteers, working together. They were friends. Part of her brothers' lives.

Confident of their place in the family.

Ellery backed toward the door. "I shouldn't take up any more of your time. I'm sure you have a million things to do before the tea starts."

Instead of returning to their work, the women fell into step with Ellery as she retraced her steps through the maze of bookcases to the main lobby.

"Are you sure you can't stay?" Maddie asked. "It's only fair you get to sample some of the food you made."

In her mind's eye, Ellery saw Carter pop a scone in his mouth. Heard the low, masculine hum of appreciation that had dared her to tease him a little.

She hadn't expected him to respond in kind.

Her heart did that freefall thing again.

"I can't. I'm sorry." Ellery made herself say the words. "I'm actually checking out this morning—"

"Miss El'ry!"

Ellery turned at the sound of a familiar voice and saw Bea crossing the lobby at full tilt. She launched herself into Ellery's arms a split second before a middle-aged woman wearing a denim dress and tennis shoes caught up to her.

Seeing the distressed look on Bea's face, Ellery gathered the little girl closer. "I thought you were at school today."

"The kindergarten class came over to participate in the children's activity during the open house today." Maddie glanced at the teacher. "But I believe Mrs. Larson sent home a note asking the parents to pick them up here afterward?"

The woman looked a little affronted that Maddie had to ask. "I certainly did."

"But Daddy's late." Bea's lower lip quivered.

"He took your grandma to the clinic this morning, remember?" Ellery gave Bea's shoulders a reassuring squeeze. "Sometimes it takes a while to get in to see the doctor."

Mrs. Larson's expression softened. "I have a mandatory staff meeting, but Bea is welcome to come back to the school with me and wait in the office until he arrives."

At the word *office* Bea's lips drooped even more.

"Or…" Ellery silently changed her plans again. "She can hang out with me."

Lily grinned. "That's a great idea! Ellery is a family friend, so Carter won't mind."

Ellery wasn't so sure about that.

Because the truth was, she didn't know where she fit in Carter's life any more than she knew where she fit in her brothers'.

Being late was becoming a habit.

When Carter had arrived at the clinic with his mother, the doctor was already backlogged with patients suffering the same symptoms as his mom. He'd stopped at the pharmacy after dropping her off at the inn, only to discover the crowd standing in line for prescriptions rivaled that of the clinic's waiting room.

Carter pushed open the double doors and headed straight for the colorful partitions that separated the children's area from the rest of the library.

There was no sign of Bea. No sign of *anyone*.

"Deputy Bristow." Maddie Montgomery emerged from behind a wall of bookcases. The dress she wore should have looked out of place in Castle Falls—and, if Carter were being honest, this century—but it fit the quiet librarian with the shy smile.

He wasn't the only one who'd been surprised when Maddie and Aiden had announced their engagement last month. A librarian who preferred velvet and lace and an avid outdoorsman whose wardrobe consisted of flannel shirts and jeans.

Complete opposites, but for some strange reason, Carter could see it working. Maybe because they loved each other *and* Castle Falls.

"I'm sorry I'm late," Carter said. "I had to stop by the pharmacy on my way over." He scanned the lobby once again. "Did Mrs. Larsen take Bea back to school?"

Maddie shook her head. "She's at The Happy Cow—"

"With Ellery."

Lily Kane and Anna Leighton had joined Maddie. Formed a semi-circle around Carter, trapping him in place with their oh-so-friendly smiles.

"Mom and Gran are serving hot chocolate ice cream with peppermint whipped cream," Anna said. "They spent weeks trying to come up with a new flavor and I told Ellery it was on the house."

"Thanks to her, the tea was a success," Lily added. "How long is she staying in Castle Falls?"

The same question that had been buzzing around inside of Carter's head like a pesky mosquito for days.

"I have no idea." He inched toward the door.

The semi-circle inched with him.

"Ellery and Bea seemed to have bonded…" A question dangled at the end of Lily's sentence.

A question Carter wasn't about to answer. Sunni Mason had earned a reputation in town as a matchmaker and it wouldn't surprise him a bit if she'd recruited more members.

"Bea gets along with everyone," he said evenly, blocking out the image of Ellery sitting on the bed next to his daughter. Taking over the nightly routine with the same breezy confidence in which she'd taken over the kitchen.

Nope. He wasn't going to think about the kitchen. Or how adorable Ellery had looked when she'd accused him of stealing.

"Ellery mentioned that Karen wasn't feeling well this weekend," Lily said. "Is she doing better today?"

Carter frowned. He wasn't sure he wanted to answer that one, either. He preferred to keep his personal and professional life separate, but for reasons he couldn't comprehend, the Kane brothers and their significant others cheerfully ignored the line between the two. And his frowns.

"Not recovering as fast as she'd like," Carter admitted. "She takes on a lot this time of year."

Like fostering horses. And church-sponsored events.

His hand closed around the doorknob.

"God always knows what we need," Anna said softly. "It's a blessing Ellery has been there to help out."

A blessing for Carter's mom. And even for Bea.

But Carter?

He didn't *want* to need anyone again.

Chapter Fourteen

Judging from the number of people crowded inside The Happy Cow when Ellery and Bea arrived, half the town must have marked this event on their calendars.

The whimsical decor on the outside of the building was reflected inside the ice cream parlor. Bistro-style tables and chairs in an array of pastel colors were scattered around the small dining area. A large sign behind the old-fashioned cash register encouraged customers to Keep Calm and Add Sprinkles.

Ellery ushered Bea to a table for two in the corner and while Bea tunneled through layers of hot fudge and peppermint whipped cream, tried to hide her growing concern.

Carter still hadn't shown up.

"How is everything?" A middle-aged woman with auburn hair paused beside the table.

"Yummy!" Bea said at once.

The woman laughed. "That's what I like to hear." She turned her attention to Ellery. "When you're finished, feel free to go upstairs and take a look around. There are some beautiful pieces if you're looking for Christmas gifts." She lowered her voice. "And I don't get a commission to say that, either! If you find something you love, bring it down and I'll ring it up for you."

Karen had mentioned how much she liked jewelry. Maybe Ellery could find something to brighten her day after the doctor appointment.

Bea finished her ice cream and they climbed a wooden staircase leading to the second floor.

Ellery wasn't sure what she expected to find, but the spacious room on the other side of the gauze curtains strung across the doorway rivaled the specialty boutiques Ellery had visited while traveling with her parents. Natural light poured through the wall of glass overlooking the main street.

The space was family-friendly, too. Bins filled with large wooden beads and colorful string had been set out on a low table, perfectly sized for children. Bea gravitated toward it immediately while Ellery wandered through the displays.

All the jewelry, from the delicate gold and silver chains draped like tinsel on birch branch centerpieces, to the tiny charms that filled rustic wooden bowls, reflected God's creation.

A photo in a rustic frame near the cash register caught Ellery's eye. Anna Leighton, her copper-haired twins… and Liam.

Someone had written "Anna's Inspiration" underneath the photograph, but judging from the expression on Liam's face, the words were true for her brother, too.

Ellery's gaze shifted to a sheaf of brochures tucked in the hand-thrown vase beside it. Even before she reached for one, before she saw a picture of a vintage canoe, she knew what business they were advertising.

Castle Falls Outfitters.

Ellery studied the photos on the front page with the intensity of someone who'd found a treasure map, searching for clues that would tell her more about her brothers.

The brochure looked professional, the company logo superimposed over the hand-drawn sketch of an oak tree, its branches stretching from border to border. The base of the trunk separated into roots anchored in the riverbank.

Ellery was about to turn the page when the floorboards outside the studio creaked. She glanced over her shoulder but even before the curtains parted, she knew it was Carter.

She fumbled to replace the brochure and it slipped between her fingers instead. Ellery watched it sail through the air as if it were riding some invisible, mischievous current that had taken control before being deposited at Carter's feet.

Naturally, he bent down and picked it up. "Interested in canoeing?"

Ellery suppressed a groan. She was surrounded by beautiful, hand-crafted jewelry, and Carter had caught her reading a travel brochure.

"It mentioned gift certificates," Ellery stammered. She glanced at Bea but the little girl who usually greeted her daddy with an exuberant hug remained at the table, engrossed in threading wooden beads onto a length of purple string. "Have you ever gone on one of their excursions?"

"No." Carter closed the distance between them in three strides and handed her the brochure. The crisp scent of snow and some woodsy masculine soap stirred the air. "But they haven't been offering those for very long."

Ellery tried to hide her confusion. "I thought you said that Brendan and his brothers took over the business when they were teenagers."

"Building canoes, yes," Carter said. "Rich and Sunni Mason lived here for years and had a strong connection with Castle Falls. They held special events on the river and encouraged church groups and families to take advantage of their property. All that changed after Rich died.

"I'm not sure who made the decision, but the next summer, they shut down the face-to-face contact with customers and the community to expand their business online. I wasn't around when all that happened, but I remember Mom was disappointed she couldn't send guests their way anymore. It was only a year or so ago they opened the doors and began to offer day trips and overnight campouts again."

"A year," Ellery murmured. Months before Aiden's accident. "Do you know why?"

Carter shrugged. "I'm just speculating here, but Lily worked in advertising before she moved to Castle Falls. It could be part of a new marketing plan."

Because the business wasn't doing well?

The question sprang into Ellery's mind, another sign that Jameson's warning about motives had taken root. But having met the women who'd willingly become part of her brothers' lives, Ellery found it difficult to believe the three men hadn't come to peace with whatever had happened in their past.

Was it wrong for her to want the same?

Ellery's gaze dropped to the brochure again and the pensive look that skimmed across her pretty face packed more of a punch than her smiles.

If it had been June and not December, Carter would be tempted to call Aiden and schedule a trip down the river himself.

A side effect of sleep deprivation. Had to be.

"It must be challenging to own a small business here." Ellery tucked the brochure back in the jar.

Carter couldn't argue with that. His mom lived it every day.

"Tourism is like farming. It's dependent on things you can't control," he said. "The weather. The economy. People have to be creative if they want to draw people here. With the lack of restaurants in the area, some people thought Anna should have expanded The Happy Cow instead of turning this space into a working studio for her jewelry business."

"It's beautiful," Ellery said softly. "I imagine that tourists would want to purchase a souvenir when they visit the area, too."

Carter wondered if Anna's designs appealed to Ellery. The diamond studs in her ears probably cost more than a county deputy's monthly take-home pay.

"Look what I made, Daddy!" Bea hopped up from the table and scampered over to them. "There's one for Gramma and one for Miss El'ry."

Ellery didn't bat an eye when she was presented with Bea's newest creation, a beaded bracelet that showcased her favorite color. Pink.

"I love it." She slipped it over her wrist. "And I know your Gramma will love the one you made for her, too."

Bea beamed a smile. "Can we bring her some ice cream, too?"

"No ice cream today," Carter said. "Dr. Wallis prescribed some medicine to make her feel better, though, so it's time for us to head home and convince her to take it."

Bea latched on to Carter's hand and looked up at Ellery. "Are you coming home, too?"

"Soon." Ellery's smile looked forced. She turned to Carter. "I think I'll look around some more and then stop by the library to pick up the trays now that the tea is over."

"Thank you." Carter hadn't thought about the trays.

Another detail that would have slid through the cracks during his watch.

They parted ways at the door and Bea skipped along at Carter's side, pointing out the window displays. One was a giant calendar, reminding Carter that Christmas was right around the corner.

He opened the back door of the SUV and helped buckle Bea into her booster before closing the door.

"Carter!" A hand clamped down on Carter's shoulder and although he'd been out of active duty for several years now, every nerve ending in Carter's body went on high alert.

He exhaled, turned around…slowly…and nodded at the man who'd stopped to greet him. "Pastor."

Seth Tamblin might have earned the title, but Carter had always thought the guy didn't really look the part. New Life Fellowship's head shepherd preferred sweatshirts, jeans and tennis shoes over a suit and tie.

"I talked to Karen last week, but if there's anything else she needs, please tell her to let Rebecca or me know." The pastor grinned. "Everyone is thrilled we have an actual barn for the live nativity. Last year we had to cancel the whole thing because the temperature was too cold for man *and* beast."

The live… Carter stared at him.

He'd totally forgotten Karen had agreed to host the event.

"Mom is sick," Carter said bluntly. "I'm not sure it's going to work out this year, either."

Seth frowned. "I hope it's nothing serious. Several of our senior members have been hospitalized with pneumonia recently."

Carter took another step away from the SUV so Bea wouldn't overhear their conversation.

"Dr. Wallis described it as a virus, but he's concerned there might be complications if she doesn't follow his orders."

And Carter knew his mom would do everything she could to keep the promise she'd made to Pastor Seth and wear herself out in the process.

"We'll keep her in our prayers," Seth said. "And if there's anything I can do, Carter, please give me a call."

Carter was tempted to tell the pastor he could start looking for an alternate venue for the live nativity, but first he had to convince a certain innkeeper it was the only option.

He hopped into the driver's seat, and Bea leaned forward as far as the safety straps would allow.

"Can we visit Sugar after we give Gramma her medicine, Daddy?"

Visiting Sugar had somehow infiltrated his day, much the way Christmas carols had taken over his favorite radio station.

Carter's hands tightened on the steering wheel as he pulled away from the curb.

How was Bea going to react when the horse went to its new home? She talked about Sugar as if it were already a member of the family.

"I suppose." Because really, what else could Carter say? Bea wouldn't understand his reasons for refusing.

You don't want Bea to be afraid to love.

Ellery's words somehow escaped from the lockbox in Carter's memory and went straight for the heart.

It was his job to protect Bea from harm. Physical *and* emotional.

Ellery wouldn't understand. And only a person who'd never experienced a gut-wrenching loss, one that changed the landscape of your soul, would encourage you to venture into that barren land and give it another try.

"It's starting to snow!" Bea practically levitated out of her booster seat. "That's in my book, too, Daddy!"

Carter wasn't sure what book she was talking about. Bea came home from the library with a backpack full every week. But right now, he'd prefer to read about snow than deal with the real stuff.

He parked behind the inn, came around to the back seat and lifted Bea down. She flitted down the walkway, head tilted toward the sky, trying to catch snowflakes on her tongue.

"Run upstairs and change out of your school clothes," Carter called after her.

He bent down to collect the jumble of hats and mittens that mysteriously collected in the back hallway this time of year and put them away before making his way to the front desk to check for messages.

At least the number of guests tended to decline during the month of December. Carter wasn't sure what he'd do if all the guest rooms were filled. The "bed" part of the inn he could handle. The breakfast part...not so much. Cold cereal and toast were the staples of his culinary repertoire.

"Daddy?" Bea appeared at the top of the stairs. "Gramma's awake!" She called down in a whisper loud enough to guarantee it was true before darting away again.

Carter hiked up the stairs to the family suite with the doctor's prescription and an apology.

"Sorry this took so long. The line at the pharmacy was practically out the door." He set the pill down on the nightstand. "How are you feeling?"

"Better, now." Karen's gaze shifted to something—or, more appropriately, *someone*—in the doorway. Her fingers fluttered in a wave. "Don't get too close, sweetheart. I don't want you to get sick, too."

Bea lingered just inside the door, rocking from foot to foot. "When are you going to get up?"

"Soon." Karen mustered a smile. "Tell me what you did today."

Bea began to tick things off on her fingers. "I went to the lib'ary with my class and Miss Maddie's helper read the stories this time because she had to make tea. Daddy was late so Miss El'ry took me to The Happy Cow for ice cream."

Karen's head rolled toward Carter, a question in her eyes.

"I was late for that, too," he admitted.

"You're working too hard." Karen's smile frayed at the edges, and Carter recognized guilt when he saw it.

"I have a great helper." He winked at Bea. "And once we finish our chores, we're going to take a walk down to the barn."

Bea pressed her fingers against her mouth, threw her arm out and sent a kiss sailing across the room. "Love you, Gramma."

Karen blew one back. "Love you, too."

She sank against the pillow the moment Bea disappeared. Carter would have made his exit, too, but his mom held up one finger, signaling him to wait.

"Can I get you something else?"

"Information." A spark of humor flared in Karen's eyes. "Did you talk to Maddie? What did she say about the tea?"

Actually, the librarian and her friends had seemed more interested in talking about Ellery, but Carter wasn't about to admit that.

"Everything went well." Carter paused, choosing his next words with care. "I ran into Pastor Seth when I was in town. He asked if you needed anything for the live nativity."

"I don't know what to do." Karen's groan morphed into a cough that sent ripples through the comforter on the bed.

"Dr. Wallis said that most people who catch this particular virus turn a corner in a few days, but even if that happens, I have guests checking in before Liam and Anna's wedding and menus to plan. Baking for Christmas…" Her voice trailed off.

"So, the wisest thing to do is tell Seth you won't be able to host it this year," Carter finished.

Karen looked torn but finally dipped her chin in a weak nod. "I know you're right, but I feel terrible, Carter. And Bea is going to be so disappointed. She was so excited when I told her there were going to be real sheep in the barn."

No one had said anything about sheep.

"I'll call Seth. He knows you wouldn't cancel if there was any other option." Carter squeezed her hand. "And don't worry about Bea. I took the rest of the week off from work so she doesn't have to go to a sitter."

"The rest of the *week*?"

Carter's lips twisted. "The office coordinator had the same reaction. You'd think I never took a vacation day."

"You don't."

"It's fine. *We're* fine. And you will be, too," Carter promised. "But you have to follow Dr. Wallis's instructions."

Karen puffed a sigh. "I will."

Before Carter reached the door, she called out to him.

"Carter? One more thing."

He paused, looked over his shoulder. "Okay."

"I know you prefer to stay in the background…but don't forget we have a guest."

Carter almost laughed.

As much as he'd like to, he had a feeling that forgetting about Ellery Marshall would be next to impossible.

Chapter Fifteen

Ellery heard the soft tread of footsteps down the hall and her traitorous heart fell into rhythm with the beat even before Carter walked into the kitchen.

His gaze swept over the hedge of brown paper bags lined up on the island. "What's all this?"

"I took a screenshot of Karen's grocery list and picked up a few things at the store on my way—" Ellery almost said *home* "—back here."

"A few things?" Carter's lips twitched. "It looks like there's enough food to take us through the winter."

"Through the end of the week at least." Ellery tried on a smile and hoped Carter didn't notice it didn't quite fit right. "Karen planned to do a lot of baking this week, so I doubled up on some of the pantry staples."

Carter reached into one of the brown paper bags and pulled out a small plastic container. Shot a look of disbelief at Ellery. "Glitter is a staple?"

"They're sprinkles," Ellery corrected. "For decorating Christmas cookies."

Carter inspected it more closely. "Anything that looks like it glows in the dark can't possibly be edible."

"Not only edible, but delicious."

Carter didn't look convinced but he set the container on the counter and took a quick inventory of the rest of her purchases. "I don't see any frozen pizza."

He was teasing her. Wasn't he? It was hard to tell when the man didn't crack a smile.

"Um...no. I saw pizza on the list and bought the ingredients to make them from scratch."

"I'm pretty sure Mama Francesca follows the same recipe before she distributes them to grocery stores all over the world."

Definitely teasing her.

Now would be the time to confess that she was leaving, but Ellery found it impossible to talk when she couldn't breathe.

Carter must have felt the change in the air, too, because he frowned.

Bea skipped into the kitchen. She'd changed into bib overalls and a turtleneck, her pigtails adorably askew. "Whatcha doing?"

Ellery was wondering the same thing. But Carter—bless the man and his "just the facts" conversational style—didn't seem to have trouble answering the question.

"Putting away groceries."

Bea went up on her tiptoes and began removing cans from a bag. "I'll help!"

"I believe those belong on the second shelf of the pantry," Carter said.

Bea tipped her head back. "I can't reach that high."

"Really? Are you sure?" Carter swept his daughter off her feet and lifted her in the air, holding her steady while she carefully placed a can of tomatoes on the shelf.

Father's and daughter's palms connected in a victorious high five.

"We need another one, Miss El'ry!" Bea instructed.

"Coming right up."

Together they formed a small but efficient assembly line.

The simple, everyday task of putting away groceries, working alongside Carter, shouldn't have felt so normal. So...right.

Neither should this unexpected—and undeniable—attraction to Carter.

"Those go in the refrigerator!" Bea chortled.

Ellery looked down. Felt the heat rush into her cheeks when she realized she'd been about to hand Carter a bag of carrots.

"Of course they do." Ellery expelled a weak laugh to cover her mistake and promptly made another when she dared a look at Carter and saw the speculative look in his eyes.

Almost as if he were trying to figure out what had distracted her.

Bea wriggled out of Carter's arms. "Can I give one to Sugar?"

"I think she'd like that." Ellery skirted around Carter and made a beeline for the sink. "I'll wash them off first."

Even with her back to Carter, Ellery was acutely aware of his presence as he transferred the produce to the bins in the refrigerator.

Bea's strangled cry had both her and Carter whirling around.

She sat on the floor, hugging a pair of ice skates against her chest. "Are these for me?"

Oops. Ellery had forgotten that not all the bags held groceries. She'd spotted the skates in the window of a store called CJ's Variety. Made from snow white leather and sporting pink laces and sparkly pompoms, they could have been designed with Bea in mind.

"Consider them an early Christmas gift." Ellery smiled. "Do you like them?"

"They're the *bestest* ever!" Bea sprang to her feet and held them up for Carter to admire. "Now we can go skating on the pond, Daddy."

Carter's gaze bounced from the skates to the window and his jaw tightened. Ellery suddenly realized the pond was buried under several feet of snow. Snow that would have to be removed before testing out a new pair of skates. Ellery's purchase had inadvertently created more work for a man who already had too much on his plate.

Or was Carter upset that she hadn't asked permission to buy Bea a gift?

"Can I try them on, Daddy?" Bea begged.

"Maybe later." Carter tweaked a golden pigtail. "You can play outside while I shovel the walkway."

"I'll show Snowflake my skates." Bea dashed over and threw her arms around Ellery's waist. "Thankyouthankyouthankyou."

"You're welcome, sweetie." Ellery's eyes met Carter's over Bea's head but there was no sign of a thaw.

So. Not only did she have to say goodbye, she owed him an apology, too.

After Carter ushered Bea out of the kitchen, Ellery tackled a few of the things on Karen's to-do list and whipped up a simple omelet in case her appetite had returned.

She'd planned to slip in and leave the tray without disturbing Karen, but the innkeeper was sitting up in bed, her head nested in her arms.

"Karen? Are you feeling worse?" Tea sloshed over the rim of the cup as Ellery hurried to her side. "Should I call Carter?"

"No. Everything is fine." Karen tucked a limp strand of hair behind her ear. "I didn't mean to scare you. I couldn't sleep so I decided to pray instead."

Ellery nodded. She'd been doing a lot of that lately, too. In a way, she and Karen weren't so different. They were in situations where they felt helpless. Where they had to make a conscious decision to trust.

"You're a believer, aren't you? I can always tell by a person's eyes." Karen smiled. "And what they do with their hands."

It sounded like something Ellery's mom would have said. Candace Marshall lived what she believed. Everything she did flowed out of her love for God and the people He put in her path.

"Ellery, may I ask you something?"

Something in Karen's tone set off a warning alarm. "Of course."

"It's almost Christmas. Why aren't you with your family?"

It was the last question Ellery had expected but there wasn't a hint of accusation or suspicion in Karen's eyes. Only kindness.

"My parents... They died last winter. I'm an only child—" It was true and yet it wasn't. The urge to tell Karen everything welled up inside Ellery, but she forced it down, along with the lump rising in her throat. "I needed some time..." *Time to find the truth about my past. My brothers.* "So, I came here."

Karen's hand folded around hers. "I'm so sorry about your loss," she said softly. "But it's a testimony to your parents' influence that you allowed the pain to draw you closer to God rather than away from Him."

Ellery wondered if Karen was thinking about Carter.

"You said you needed peace and quiet," Karen continued. "But God knew we needed you. I've been running this inn for twenty years and I know for a fact there's never been a guest who could handle my son, my precious but active granddaughter and the menu for a high tea."

Ellery felt the color rise in her cheeks. "I enjoyed every minute of it."

Maybe too much.

"I can tell. I know a kindred soul when I see one." Karen took a sip of tea. "Which is why I want to hire you."

"*Hire* me?"

"Yes." Karen's voice was surprisingly firm for someone too weak to get out of bed. "Only for a few days. Until I get my strength back again. There will be guests arriving in the next day or two and as much as I love Carter, he is more comfortable in a squad car than the kitchen."

Ellery opened her mouth. Closed it again. She didn't know what to say.

"You don't have to decide right away." Karen squeezed Ellery's hand. "Take some time and think about it."

If Jameson were here, the attorney would say the suitcase on the floor next to Ellery's bed, packed and waiting, meant the decision to stay or leave had already been made.

But what if God had other plans?

Ellery had been praying He would show her what to do.

What if she *wasn't* supposed to leave yet?

"I won't be upset if you say no," Karen said, misinterpreting Ellery's silence for reluctance. "I realize it will change things, but right now I need someone I can trust to hold things together."

Ellery wasn't sure that person was her. Not when her dream of reuniting with the only family she had left was falling apart.

Not when she was falling for a man who'd made no secret of the fact that he didn't believe in dreams at all.

John Wayne made this look so much easier.

Carter might not be a cowboy, but he'd been trained to assess and defuse potentially volatile situations. And something in the way Sugar's ears lay flat against her head told Carter the mare wasn't too keen on sharing her stall.

"Housekeeping," he said, holding up the rake as proof. "All I need is five minutes and then you can go back to whatever it was you were doing."

Behind him, Bea giggled.

Carter was tempted to call the Kanes and complain they'd missed a spot, but he wasn't in the mood to decipher the brothers' secret code of veiled comments and knowing looks.

He tried another approach. "Bea, hand me another carrot, please."

"They're all gone."

"Resorting to bribery again?" The question, accompanied by a low laugh, brought Sugar's head around.

Carter glanced over his shoulder and the air emptied from his lungs.

Ellery had changed clothes before coming down to the barn. She always looked beautiful, but in leather boots, a pair of faded jeans and a fleece-lined coat that looked suspiciously like the one Carter had stashed in the hall closet months ago, she looked more approachable than she did in cashmere.

More…kissable.

Whoa.

Carter put those thoughts on lockdown before they could lead him into dangerous ground.

"Daddy is talking to Sugar," Bea informed Ellery in a whisper. "But she's not being a good listener."

Carter could see Ellery struggling to wrestle down a smile as she joined him in the stall.

"Hey there, girl," she crooned. "How about a little bedtime snack before we tuck you in for the night?"

The horse nickered an agreeable reply.

"Bea? Will you scoop some grain into that metal pan on top of the feed bin, please?"

Bea shot into action and returned a few moments later. She handed Ellery the pan. Sugar stretched out her neck to investigate its contents and her ears lifted in approval once again.

Ellery responded to Carter's incredulous look with an innocent shrug of her shoulders.

"Everyone likes a bedtime snack." She neatly divested Carter of the rake before he could protest. The stall was clean before Sugar finished vacuuming up the oats.

"There." Ellery ran her hand over the horse's mane before backing out of the stall. Carter followed and slid the door back into place.

"Is it okay if I give Snowflake some oats before she goes to sleep, too?" Bea asked.

"That's a great idea." Without hesitation, Ellery sprinkled a handful of the grain into the pan for Bea's snow horse.

"Stay close to the house," Carter called out of habit as she dashed for the door, the tail of her pink stocking cap lifting like a windsock, buoyed by the force that was Bea.

The barn door closed, sealing him and Ellery inside.

Suddenly, Carter felt as jittery as a new recruit on his first underwater dive.

The pull of physical attraction he understood. The chemistry between him and Jennifer had burned as hot as a brush fire and died just as quickly. This felt different. Spending time with Ellery made Carter think about the future, not the past.

"I'll get some fresh bedding."

Sugar wasn't his responsibility, but Carter had to do something to keep those unruly thoughts in line.

Ellery stepped in front of him and blocked his path. "I'm sorry."

Carter frowned. "For…"

"The ice skates. I should have asked you before I gave them to Bea," Ellery said. "But pink laces and pompoms? I couldn't resist. Your reaction when you saw them… It was obvious that I… I'd overstepped."

Chapter Sixteen

And here Carter thought he'd become such an expert on hiding his emotions.

He pivoted toward the window and looked outside to make sure his daughter hadn't wandered from view. Bea was deep in conversation with her snow horse, gently patting the dishmop mane, mimicking Ellery's affectionate gesture toward Sugar a few minutes ago.

"There's no need to apologize," Carter said, hoping that would be the end of it. "You didn't do anything wrong."

Ellery moved closer and Carter felt his gut tighten.

How was it that she'd picked up on some subtle, nonverbal cue when they were in the kitchen and totally missed Carter's need to put a little space between them now?

"What, then?" Ellery touched his arm and Carter's heart short-circuited like a faulty string of lights on a Christmas tree. "Is it because you have to clear snow off the pond for a rink?"

Carter wasn't sure he could tell Ellery that he was angry with himself, not her.

Ellery's purchase wasn't about crossing boundaries or adding another project on an already packed to-do list. It was pure, undiluted guilt.

"How did you know Bea wanted skates?"

Ellery's brow furrowed as if she were trying to decide whether it was a trick question.

"Page three in *Isabella's Best Christmas Ever*?"

"Isabella's what?" Had he missed something else?

"The book Bea wrote."

There was his answer.

"She didn't show that one to me."

Ellery didn't look horrified or disgusted that Carter had had no idea his daughter was an author.

"It was an activity at the library," she explained. "Maddie asked all the children to write down the things that would make this the best Christmas ever."

Carter closed his eyes for a moment. It was the wishing bell all over again.

"I'm almost afraid to ask."

"Why?"

Carter was used to asking the questions. He wasn't sure whether to be amused or annoyed that Ellery had turned the tables on him.

"When we got home from the parade that night, Bea told me she'd wished for a real horse that looks like Snowflake…"

Understanding dawned in Ellery's eyes. "Sugar."

"How do you explain a coincidence to someone with an imagination like Bea? Someone who thinks the world is this beautiful place when you know…" Carter pushed aside the dark images that flooded his mind. "When you know it *isn't*. I do my best to protect her but—"

Carter felt like he was failing at that, too.

"Protecting Bea is part of your job as a father," Ellery said softly. "But it doesn't mean that you stand on the perimeter of her life and keep watch. Bea needs you to be *with* her."

Carter was afraid of that, too.

"Mom is more comfortable with the sunny side of life," he muttered. "I'm sure you've figured out I'm not wired that way."

"I figured out you use that as an excuse to keep your distance from people." Ellery met his eyes. "Including your own daughter."

Had Carter really thought Ellery was as harmless as one of Bea's stuffed ponies? Because right now, every word she said fell like a hammer blow.

"Bea is…amazing. There's too much at stake. I don't want to make a mistake and fail at parenting, too."

"You *will* make mistakes, Carter. You're human. But I'd rather make mistakes than have regrets. And you…you have a lot to give."

The fact Ellery was extending grace that Carter didn't deserve somehow made it worse.

"Not according to my ex-wife."

Had he really just said that out loud? Judging from the expression on Ellery's face, he had.

"She was wrong." Ellery sounded so certain, Carter was tempted to believe her.

"The divorce papers Jennifer handed me when I told her that I wasn't going to reenlist don't exactly support that theory."

Carter hadn't meant to say that, either. What was wrong with him? He never talked about his ex-wife or the past.

"Why did you leave the Navy?"

"I wasn't going to be like my dad and choose my career over family. It was too late, though. I practically begged Jennifer to give our marriage another chance, but she'd already made up her mind." Even after three years, the sound of Jennifer's laughter when Carter had suggested they see a counselor still echoed in his memory. "She'd found someone else. Told me to stick to what I was good at because it certainly wasn't relationships."

"You gave up a career you loved for your family. You were willing to do whatever it took to save your marriage, and your ex-wife walked away from her husband and child. I'm not a detective, Carter, but it appears to me that *she* was the one who wasn't good at relationships."

A part of Carter wanted to absorb that as truth, but his own father had left without a backward glance when Carter wasn't much older than Bea. Didn't that make him the common denominator in both situations?

"Ask me about policy and procedures and protocol, and it's all good. But Bea…" Carter's throat tightened. "She's…amazing. She deserved so much more and got stuck with me."

"Bea doesn't see it that way. She loves your mom but she needs you, too. And she doesn't care what's under the Christmas tree. All the things Bea wrote down in her book aren't really things at all. She wants time with the people she loves. She wants…"

"Wants?" Carter prompted when Ellery suddenly ran out of steam.

"Her daddy to smile more."

If Carter had been questioning whether his heart was in working order anymore, he got his answer. Because Ellery's words hit their target dead center.

"I smile."

"No." Ellery contradicted him. Again. "You really don't. Your lips…" Her gaze dropped for a moment and bounced back up. She cleared her throat. "They twitch a little at the corners, but that's about it."

"Twitch?"

"Don't get me wrong," Ellery added quickly. "It's very, um, attractive. The twitch. But you need to practice a little more."

"I need to practice. Smiling."

"Uh-huh. It's like you're holding back in that area, too. It's not always about control. Sometimes you have to… let go."

Carter decided to take her advice. He took a step closer.

Ellery's startled expression and the surge of color in her cheeks brought a smile to Carter's lips. He gave it free rein.

"Like this?"

"That's…good." Ellery began to back up, and Carter caught her hand before she made contact with a rusty nail protruding from the wall.

"Your ears are already pierced, so…"

Ellery laughed, the sound low and sweet, and Carter threaded his fingers through hers, locking them together.

Her hands were delicate. Her skin as soft as satin.

Carter's mind made the leap on its own, wondering if her lips were, too.

He couldn't stop himself from drawing Ellery deeper into the circle of his arms any more than he could have stopped his next breath. Surprise flared in Ellery's eyes and then Carter saw something else take its place. Something that made him forget all about the past.

"Ellery…"

The snap of a car door jolted them apart. Jolted Carter back to reality.

"Guests?" Ellery asked.

Carter looked out the window and sighed.

More like trouble.

Ellery's heart, still in recovery mode, took another roller-coaster dive when she looked outside and saw the black pickup truck with the Castle Falls logo painted on the side.

The driver's-side door swung open and Aiden hopped down from the cab. He jogged around the hood to the passenger side of the vehicle and extended a hand to Sunni Mason, guiding her safely to the ground.

Lord? I'm not sure I can take much more.

Carter muttered something under his breath as he strode toward the door.

Ellery contemplated staying in the barn, but if Aiden and Sunni had returned to check on Sugar, she'd end up trapped in polite conversation, pretending everything was fine.

And pretending was beginning to extract a heavy price.

She followed Carter out of the barn just in time to see Liam's lean frame unfold from the back seat.

Ellery wasn't sure if it was the aftershock from being in Carter's arms or seeing two of her brothers again that was responsible for the sudden wobble in her step.

At least Carter didn't notice and reach out to steady her this time. Which was probably a good thing because Sunni Mason had already drawn her own conclusion about them the night they'd visited her booth at the carnival.

A conclusion that had seemed far beyond the realm of possibility at the time.

But now…

Ellery hoped the woman would attribute the burst of color in her cheeks to the snow swirling in the air.

"Mom wanted me to call and give you a heads-up we were on our way over," Aiden said cheerfully. "But I knew you wouldn't answer the phone, so here we are." He punctuated the statement with an affectionate thump to Carter's back.

The few times Carter had talked about Ellery's brothers, he'd made it seem as if their relationship was more professional than personal. Her brothers obviously viewed things differently.

Bea dashed over to greet their visitors and Aiden swept her off the ground. "Hey, Goldilocks."

Carter frowned when Aiden set Bea on the ledge of his broad shoulder. "Didn't you break that arm?"

"What did I tell you?" Aiden tossed a grin at Liam. "He really does care."

But Liam wasn't paying any attention to Aiden. He was looking at her.

"Ellery. It's nice to see you again."

The friendly greeting belied the sudden intensity of his gaze, and Ellery suddenly wanted to bolt for the safety of the inn.

What exactly did Liam see? The smudges of indigo blue in the palette of Ellery's eyes that were a perfect match to his? The similarities in features carved from the same genetic tree?

Or were there traces of their biological mother in Ellery's smile? The way she wore her hair?

"Liam." Ellery dipped her head and zipped up her coat another two inches in order to avoid his gaze.

Her emotions simmered too close to the surface to deal with this unexpected visit from her brothers, but Ellery knew she'd only draw more attention if she gave in to the urge to flee.

She pressed out a smile for Aiden and Sunni. "Did you come out to check on Sugar again?"

"Not this time." Sunni held up a large plastic container. "I heard Karen was under the weather, so I brought her some of my homemade chicken noodle soup."

"I'm sure she'll appreciate it." Carter reached for the soup, but Sunni didn't relinquish possession.

"I'll find my way to the kitchen, drop this off and then pop in and say a quick hello to Karen."

"I don't know if that's a good idea." Carter frowned. "You don't want to expose yourself to anything contagious." Aiden looped his arm around Sunni's shoulders. "Mom never gets sick."

Mom.

Ellery didn't know how Sunni Mason had come to adopt her brothers, but like Candace Marshall, it was a choice she'd made out of love. And watching how Aiden treated Sunni, it was clear that love was returned.

Gratitude that her brothers had formed such a strong bond with the woman who'd adopted them was overshadowed by another question that rolled through Ellery's mind.

One of the things she'd admired most about her adoptive parents was the way they reached out to people in need. Based on what Carter had said and the things Ellery had discovered about their biological father, her brothers had definitely fallen into that category.

Why hadn't her parents adopted them, too?

Sunni's warm laugh brought Ellery back to reality.

"I texted Karen before we got here and asked permission," the woman told Carter, not the least bit intimidated by his frown. "I promise I won't stay long!"

Carter gave in with a reluctant nod and opened the door. Light spilled from the inn and cast a mother-of-pearl glow on the shadows and the snow.

"We gave Sugar a bedtime snack," Bea announced from her perch on Aiden's shoulder. "And Miss El'ry cleaned up her mess."

"Is that so?" Aiden aimed his signature grin in Ellery's direction as he set Bea down on the ground again. "I'd say our timing was perfect, then."

Chapter Seventeen

Aiden's teasing comment triggered a flashback and it took all of Carter's self-control to push aside the image of Ellery's face from when he'd drawn her into his arms.

Perfect timing?

Or the absolute worst?

The jury was still out as far as Carter was concerned.

"I'm glad Sugar has a comfortable stall because it's getting pretty nippy out here, isn't it, Liam?" Aiden said.

"Nippy," Liam agreed.

Carter was about to suggest the cab of their truck was still warm but with Karen indisposed, he was in charge of hospitality.

"Do you want to come inside, too?"

"That would be great." Liam speared his hands in his front pockets, a casual gesture that immediately roused Carter's suspicions. "There's something Aiden and I wanted to discuss with you."

"And it would probably be best if you were sitting down," Aiden added.

Now he knew why Sunni hadn't come alone. But Carter had no one to blame but himself. He'd walked right into their trap.

Everyone filed into the lobby and Carter got the impression Ellery would have continued walking and headed right up the stairs if Aiden hadn't stepped in front of her.

"You should stay, Ellery. We might need a mediator."

Carter expected Ellery to succumb to the youngest Kane's charm like every other female within a hundred-mile radius, but he couldn't help but feel a perverse stab of pleasure when she looked hesitant.

Looked at *him.*

"I don't mind if you don't." Carter bent down and helped Bea take off her coat and boots. "Go play in the family room for a few minutes, okay, Izzybea?"

"Is this a growned-up talk?"

"It appears that way."

"Okay." Bea's sigh reflected her feelings on the matter before she trudged away.

The gathering room was vacant, so Carter motioned them inside. Liam and Aiden claimed the chairs by the coffee table and Ellery took a position near the fireplace. Aiden's teasing comment about Carter needing a chair was the reason he chose *not* to sit down.

"If this is about Tim and Justin Wagner, I won't say I told you so," Carter said.

Aiden and Liam exchanged a glance.

"It isn't…and I think you just did," Liam said drily. "Pastor Seth said he got a voice mail from you this afternoon, canceling the live nativity."

Carter nodded. No surprise the news had gotten out already. "Mom and I talked about it this morning and under the circumstances, the best thing to do is move it to a different location."

"Except there isn't one," Aiden said, his expression turning serious for once.

"Correct me if I'm wrong, but hasn't your church always hosted the live nativity in the past?"

"Yes." It was Liam who answered the question. "Some of the men converted an old lean-to behind the church into a stable about five years ago. But the number of people attending every year continues to grow, and you know how unpredictable the weather can be around Christmas for outdoor activities.

"If it was a church event, we could let the congregation know there's been a last-minute change or cancellation, but the Evergreen's address has been featured on every poster, community calendar and radio spot for weeks. It would be impossible to let everyone know about a last-minute change in venue."

"People look forward to the live nativity every year." Aiden leaned forward, braced his hands on his knees. "It's more than an event. It's a reminder that the best gift came from heaven."

The sincerity in his tone was unmistakable but Carter couldn't ignore the facts.

"I understand your dilemma," he said. "Here's mine. I'm keeping an eye on the inn and Bea started Christmas vacation this morning. With my mom out of commission, I can't devote any time to setting up the barn." Carter shot Aiden a pointed look. "Not to mention it's already occupied."

"Sugar is on the pro side of the list." Aiden grinned. "You already have one of the animals. Liam is in charge of setup and will show off his mad carpentry skills. You won't have to do a thing."

"Liam as in Liam Kane?" Carter lifted a brow. "The guy who's getting married on Christmas Eve? The day after the live nativity?"

"Yup." The groom-to-be got that goofy lovesick look on his face again. "I have Anna's blessing. Cassie and Chloe are part of the angel choir and they've been practicing their song for weeks."

"Brendan offered to pitch in, too," Aiden added, as if having another Kane involved ranked on the "pro" side, too. "And if you need help around the inn, just say the word."

"Help with what?"

"Anything." Aiden rolled his eyes at Liam. "You wouldn't think we'd have to explain this to a former Navy SEAL. Think of us as part of your unit. We have your back, bro."

Carter should have sat down. Because the matter-of-fact statement almost took him out at the knees.

His *unit*?

He thought he'd kept a professional distance since Aiden's accident but apparently—and Carter didn't know how, where, or when—the Kane brothers had decided he was a friend.

A fragment of his conversation with Ellery shifted in Carter's memory.

You keep everyone at a distance.

For Carter, maintaining boundaries with people in the community fell into the same category as putting on his bullet-proof vest. It was the smart thing to do. People inevitably bent or broke the rules, and if that person was a friend, issuing a ticket or a warrant for an arrest was difficult.

So was responding to the scene of an accident and performing chest compressions on the buddy you'd gone fishing with the day before.

"It's not just the barn." Carter sensed he was losing the battle, but he couldn't go down without one last fight. "From what I understand, Mom was going to provide refreshments for everyone and she's pretty picky about what comes out of her kitchen."

Carter hadn't expected them to cave, but he hadn't expected the brothers to exchange a triumphant fist-bump, either.

"That's where Ellery comes in," Liam said.

"Ellery?" Her name came out a little louder than Carter intended.

"She's your secret weapon." Aiden rubbed his hand against his stomach. "Maddie might have dropped off some leftovers from that tea thingy today."

Carter's gaze shifted to Ellery, too. She didn't look like a secret weapon at the moment. She looked like a deer caught in the headlights of an eighteen-wheeler.

"You're forgetting something important. Ellery doesn't work here. She's a guest."

Ellery caught her lip between her teeth in a gesture that was becoming as familiar to Carter as her smile.

"That's...not completely accurate."

"What isn't completely accurate?"

"Your mom hired me to take her place in the kitchen until she's back on her feet."

Hired.

Ellery still wasn't sure who'd been more shocked by her announcement, her or Carter. Because the word kind of implied she'd already made up her mind and accepted Karen's offer.

You said you'd think about it. What were you thinking?

Ellery grabbed the chef's knife and took out her frustration on an unsuspecting tomato before tossing it into the salad bowl.

She'd taken refuge in the kitchen after Sunni and her brothers left, but the simple act of preparing a meal didn't clear her head. A half an hour later, Ellery's thoughts were still spinning.

The bleat of the kitchen timer and the buzz of her cell formed a duet that made Ellery wish she were Bea's age again. At least then she could press her hands against her ears and squeeze her eyes shut to avoid a "growned-up" talk.

Ellery should have known Jameson wouldn't be satisfied with the brief voice mail she'd left on his phone.

"Hi, Jameson."

"What is going on, Ellery? I thought you'd be home by now."

Ellery pinched the phone between her ear and her shoulder and pulled the pizza stone from the oven. "Karen is still sick, Jameson. What else could I do?"

"For starters, you could hire an entire staff to take care of the inn instead of putting yourself on the payroll."

Ellery winced. Maybe she should have left out that part of the message when she'd told Jameson she was extending her stay. Again.

"You and I both know I'm not going to accept any payment," Ellery said.

Jameson's sigh filtered through the line. "You are definitely Candace Marshall's daughter."

Yes. But she was a Kane, too.

That was what made this whole situation so complicated.

"Mom never turned her back on someone who needed help."

"There are other people who need you, too," Jameson reminded her. "What about the foundation?"

Ellery ignored a pinch of guilt. "Everything is going fine. I've been sorting through the online applications and Phil is handling the daily correspondence with our sponsors."

Philomena James's official title in the Marshall household was housekeeper, but she'd been more personal assistant and confidante to Candace while Ellery was growing up. After Ellery's parents died, Phil had supported her decision to start the Marshall Foundation and offered to help in whatever capacity was needed.

"Are you sure Karen is the only reason you decided to stay longer?" Jameson finally asked. "Because as far as the situation goes, nothing has changed."

Ellery swallowed hard.

Everything had changed.

Liam and Aiden's appeal to Carter to stick with the plan for the live nativity had blindsided Ellery.

Her brothers were believers.

Jameson would argue that there were dozens of reasons people attended church, that it wasn't indicative of a genuine faith, but the confident glow in Aiden's eyes when he'd told Carter the best gift had come from heaven said otherwise.

Ellery had learned something about Carter, too. She'd never imagined he would let his guard down. Let her see the burden of guilt he carried from his brief marriage to Jennifer. The battles still being waged inside him.

And Carter had revealed something else, too.

Something that told Ellery her unexpected, confusing and complicated feelings for a very complicated man weren't one-sided.

But did that mean he'd changed his mind about *her*?

The safest thing to do was to get in the car and try to outrun her feelings, but Ellery's heart had refused to cooperate.

"Ellery?"

Jameson's voice intruded on her thoughts.

Ellery was glad he couldn't see the blush that warmed her cheeks.

"Don't worry." She hoped Jameson wouldn't realize she'd dodged his original question. "I'll keep in touch."

"Good. Because if you don't, I might have to drive up

there and stay a few days. Make sure you're really okay," Jameson warned. "And my no sugar, no carb, no fun diet might not go over well with the other guests."

Ellery had a feeling the attorney was only half joking. Her smile faded when she hung up the phone.

For all Ellery knew, she might be a guest again, too.

Carter had gone upstairs after Sunni and her brothers left, so Ellery imagined he'd paid his mom a visit to verify her story. Convince Karen they didn't need her help.

That was the trouble. Carter didn't think he needed anyone's help.

Ellery transferred the pizza onto a tray and tucked a basket filled with warm breadsticks on the side.

The family didn't eat in the main dining room with the guests, but the large coffee table Ellery had noticed in the center of their private living room would be the perfect place to gather together for an informal meal.

She carried the tray down the short hallway and tapped on the door.

The door swung open and there stood Bea.

"Pizza!" A wide smile bloomed on the girl's face and Ellery smiled back.

At least one member of the Bristow family was happy to see her.

"I thought you might be getting hungry." Ellery carried the tray into the room and her eyes lit on Carter.

The man who worried that he would fail as a father sat on the floor, long legs stretched out in front of him, surrounded by plastic ponies.

Carter returned her gaze evenly, his thoughts shielded from view.

Okay, then. Ellery could do that, too. Maybe.

"It's not Mama Francesca's," she said. "But I hope it's a close second."

Carter herded ponies onto the rug and rose to his feet. Ellery always forgot how *tall* he was until she found herself staring at the third button on the placket of his denim shirt.

"I didn't know what you'd like to drink, so I brought apple cider." She backed toward the door. "I'll see you in the morning."

Bea's face fell. "Aren't you going to eat with us?"

"I—" While Ellery was scrambling for an excuse to decline, Carter held out an empty plate.

"Bea's right. You went to all this trouble."

"It was no trouble…but thank you." Ellery dipped her head, suddenly self-conscious. "I… I'd love to stay."

Chapter Eighteen

For how long?

The question chased through Carter's mind and he quickly put it on lockdown.

He was still trying to wrap his head around the fact that his mom had offered Ellery a job.

You're the first one to come up with a logical fix for things, Carter, Karen had said when he'd confronted her about her decision to hire Ellery. *I'm surprised you didn't think of it first.*

And what was Carter supposed to say to that?

I've been too busy thinking about kissing her?

Carter prided himself on keeping his emotions in check, but it was difficult to *stop* thinking about kissing Ellery when she sat down on the floor next to Bea, her dark hair gleaming in the firelight as she divided up the pizza.

His daughter kept up an animated monologue while they ate, which suited Carter just fine.

The boundaries were changing so quickly, it was hard to keep up. Ellery had gone from registered guest to resident chef to dinner companion in the space of a few hours.

Logical, his mom had said?

There was nothing logical about any of this.

"I'm all done!" Bea announced. "Can we have cake for dessert, El'ry?"

"I don't think Ellery can whip up a cake…" Carter saw Ellery's smile and stopped. "Can you?"

"Of course." Ellery held out her hand. "But I'll need your coffee mug."

Carter's fingers tightened around the handle. "I like my coffee mug."

"You're going to like it better when it's filled with cake." He handed it over.

"Can I help?" Bea looked up at Ellery hopefully.

Ellery put her finger to her lips. "As long as you don't tell anyone my secret family recipe."

"I promise." Bea drew a lopsided X over her heart. "Can Daddy help, too?"

"I think we'll let your daddy stay here and clean up." Ellery grinned at him over Bea's head. "He has enough classified information in his head."

Carter wasn't going to have to practice smiling. It seemed to be happening all on its own.

He tucked his hands into his pockets before he did something crazy again. Like finish what he'd started the last time he and Ellery were alone.

Carter stoked the fire again and had just finished piling the plates and wrinkled napkins on the now empty pizza stone when they returned.

Bea was in full giggle mode as Ellery returned Carter's coffee mug and handed him a spoon.

"It's chocolate, Daddy!"

"Chocolate mocha," Ellery corrected. "I didn't want to dump out that last half inch of coffee."

Was there anything Ellery couldn't do?

Carter dipped the spoon into the cake and chocolate erupted to the surface like molten lava.

"It's delicious. But how—"

"We can't tell you, 'member?" Bea said. "El'ry's mommy showed her how to make it when she was a little girl."

Once again, it occurred to Carter how little he knew about Ellery. Her background. Where she lived or what she did for a living.

And Carter had never asked. Because it was safer to assume Ellery was a spoiled trust-fund baby like Jennifer.

He'd assumed a lot of things.

"Can we make cake tomorrow, too?" Bea's spoon clattered against the bottom of the empty cup.

"Christmas cookies are on the list for tomorrow," Ellery said. "Would you like to help me decorate them?"

"Yes!"

"Bea?" Carter studied his daughter's chocolate-smeared face. "Did any of that cake end up here?" He tickled her tummy and was rewarded with a giggle. "Run upstairs and get washed up. I'll be there in a few minutes to read you a story."

"Ellery, too?"

Carter should have seen that coming.

"There are a few things I have to check on in the kitchen." Ellery broke the awkward silence and smiled at Bea. "But I promise I'll pop in and say good-night before you fall asleep."

Bea's faith in promises far outweighed Carter's. She gave Ellery a quick hug and dashed from the room.

The last log in the fireplace collapsed on itself, sending a shower of crimson sparks up the chimney. Carter grabbed a few sticks of oak from the bin to keep it going.

"We're supposed to get four inches of snow tonight…" Carter glanced over his shoulder, but Ellery had left the room as swiftly as she'd come up with a reason to avoid participating in Bea's bedtime routine.

So why did Carter feel disappointed?

That wasn't logical, either.

Neither was deliberately seeking out Ellery's company again, but Carter turned toward the kitchen instead of the stairs.

Ellery slipped on her apron again and studied the items on Karen's chalkboard calendar.

Wondered why she'd thought she could do this.

Lord, I'm going to need Your help.

And not only with her new responsibilities at the inn.

Carter hadn't said much during dinner, but Bea's laughter had filled the gaps, brought back sweet memories of what it was like to be part of a family.

Ellery had dreamed about finding her brothers, but it was this little family—Carter's family—that had worked its way into her heart.

Ellery's shoulders lifted and fell with her sigh.

"Having second thoughts?"

At the sound of Carter's voice, the chalk between Ellery's fingers snapped in half. She'd assumed he'd followed Bea upstairs.

"No." Maybe. *Yes.*

Carter sauntered into the room and Ellery stiffened. *Now* he wanted to talk.

"Are you sure?" Carter eyed the broken pieces of chalk clutched in her hand. "It's not a crime to have second thoughts about working at the inn."

Not second thoughts. Doubts about her ability to avoid her brothers until Karen could take over again.

Ellery believed in the importance of honesty, and hiding her identity was becoming more difficult with each passing day.

"There is a lot to do," Ellery admitted. "But it can't be much different than hosting a dinner party."

"A very *large* dinner party. Outdoors. With sheep."

"There were animals around the night Jesus was born and a whole lot of other things that didn't go as planned," Ellery said softly. "At least not from a human perspective. It's our expectations that get us into trouble and I'd rather be…expectant. Trust that God has everything under control and give Him room to work."

Carter stared at her, silent, and Ellery tried not to fidget under the sharpness of his gaze.

Had she overstepped again?

"What else is on the list?"

Okay. Back to business.

Ellery launched into an updated plan to divide and conquer in order to reassure Carter that she was up for the task.

"If you handle the desk and the outside chores, I'll plan meals for the guests who are coming in and serve breakfast in the morning. I already have some menu ideas for the live nativity, so I'll do the shopping for that, too…"

Carter held up his hand when Ellery paused to take a breath.

"Not that list." The smile Ellery had seen in the barn appeared again. Stole her ability to breathe. "Bea's."

Hope took wing when Ellery realized Carter was referring to the book his daughter had written.

But as much as Ellery wanted to believe he'd taken her advice about spending time with Bea to heart, only God had the power to truly change one.

But maybe—*please, Lord*—this was a start.

The next morning, after hours of tossing and turning, thoughts shifting from prayers to dreams, Ellery looked at the winter wonderland outside the kitchen window.

Four inches of new snow, as glossy and smooth as a layer of white chocolate fondant, softened the landscape and frosted the branches of the trees and the outbuildings near the pond. The thick batting of gray clouds overhead was beginning to thin, allowing the sun to peek through the seams.

A movement near the barn caught Ellery's eye.

Carter.

Much to Ellery's chagrin, he'd been awake before her. Ellery had come downstairs to start the coffee only to discover he'd gotten there first. The carafe was full and over the Christmas carols—*Christmas carols*—playing on the radio, Ellery could hear the scrape of a shovel against the walkway outside. He'd been expanding the path to the barn, every movement crisp and efficient, a reflection of the man she'd gotten to know over the course of the week.

And yet...

Ellery glanced at the chalkboard wall again.

If the words *skating rink* weren't written in tiny letters in the next square on the calendar, Ellery might have convinced herself she'd dreamed the whole thing.

Carter had retreated to the family wing, but his smile had lingered in Ellery's memory long after she'd gone to bed.

"What are you looking at, El'ry?"

Ellery hadn't heard Bea enter the kitchen. She backpedaled away from the sink, hoping Carter hadn't caught her staring out the window, too.

"The snow." It was true. And much safer than admitting *your father*.

"Can I go outside and play after breakfast?" Bea scrambled onto a stool at the island. "I don't have school today."

"That's up to your daddy, sweetheart," Ellery said. Carter hadn't said when he planned to convert the pond into a skating rink, but she didn't want to spoil the surprise for Bea. "What would you like for breakfast? French toast or waffles?"

"French toast, please." Bea hadn't changed out of her pajamas yet, but Carter must have fixed her hair before he tackled the outside chores. One of Bea's pigtails was longer than the other and several golden curls had already popped free from the rubber band holding them in place.

Carter's valiant attempt sent a wave of tenderness washing through Ellery.

This was the man who was afraid he would fail his daughter.

Ellery stole one more glance out the window but Carter had disappeared from sight.

Time to focus on the task at hand.

Ellery whisked the eggs and milk in a bowl and let Bea dip slices of bread in the mixture and sprinkle them with cinnamon before they went into the pan.

Remembering what a patient teacher her mom had been in the kitchen, Ellery's thoughts drifted to Carter's ex-wife again.

Did Bea's mother realize all the precious moments she was missing out on? Did she regret her decision at all?

It was incomprehensible to Ellery that Jennifer had placed all the blame on Carter before she'd left for another man. And heartbreaking Carter thought he somehow deserved her scorn.

"May I have another piece, El'ry?" Bea held up her empty plate.

Ellery feigned astonishment. "What did you do with the first one I gave you?"

"It's right here!" Bea patted her rounded tummy.

"Mmm. I'll try to keep up." Ellery winked and slid another piece of French toast onto the little girl's plate.

While Bea finished eating, Ellery pulled up some photos of appetizers on her phone. Christmas cookies were a staple for large gatherings like a live nativity but popcorn was portable, too, and she could ask Karen about setting up a hot chocolate bar in the small outbuilding adjacent to the barn.

It occurred to Ellery that although Carter's mom wasn't well enough to do all the prep work, Karen would be the one overseeing the event.

Even if Ellery stayed, she'd be a guest once again…and a cordial stranger to her brothers.

It didn't feel like enough anymore.

The back door opened and a burst of cold air preceded Carter's entrance. The crop of goose bumps that rose on Ellery's arms was the product of the look he leveled in her direction.

Carter hadn't acknowledged what had happened between them the day before, but there was a change in the air now. An invisible, fragile connection that Ellery was afraid to name.

Bea sat up taller, her blue eyes wide with curiosity, when he set a large plastic bin on the floor.

"What's in there, Daddy?"

Carter beckoned her over. "Take a look."

Bea abandoned what was left of her breakfast, dropped to her knees in front of the bin, and peered at the contents. Her rosebud mouth formed an O of wonder. "Skates!"

"I knew these were collecting dust somewhere." Carter pulled out a pair of skates and held up them up in front of Ellery. "I wore these when I was about fifteen, but with insulated socks they'll probably fit you."

"Me?" Ellery squeaked. "Those are hockey skates."

"Afraid they won't coordinate with your pink scarf?"

No, afraid she was going to fall flat on her rump in front of witnesses.

"Black is neutral. It goes with everything...and I haven't skated in years."

"You have to, El'ry!" Bea chimed in. "Don't you want to see if my new skates work?"

There was only one answer to that question.

"Definitely."

"I'll be right back, Daddy! I'm going to get dressed." Bea dashed out of the kitchen and Ellery heard the thump of her feet against the stairs.

"You don't mind, do you?" Carter asked.

"Of course not." He'd made clearing a spot on the pond a priority. Ellery was the one who'd given Bea the skates. It seemed only fair that she supervised while Carter finished his work outside.

Fifteen minutes later, Ellery was kneeling in the snow, helping Bea put her skates on.

Underneath the covering of snow, the ice shone like glass.

"Careful!" Ellery took hold of Bea's hand as they wobbled onto the rink and took a slow, careful lap around the perimeter of the pond.

Ellery was just getting the hang of it when Bea spun around, taking Ellery with her.

"There's Daddy!"

Ellery watched Carter disappear into the small stone outbuilding adjacent to the barn. He emerged a few minutes later carrying three brooms. With the paint sloughing off the wooden handles and half the bristles missing, they looked as old as the building where they'd been stored.

Carter must have come to the same conclusion as Ellery. If the number of people attending the live nativity was as high as Brendan projected, they needed more space. Which meant Carter had to clean out one of the outbuildings he'd wanted to tear down.

He strode toward the bench that overlooked the pond and Ellery almost lost her balance all over again when she saw the pair of hockey skates draped over his shoulder.

Bea changed direction and hauled Ellery along with her. By the time they reached Carter's side, he was lacing up his skates.

He glanced up, caught them staring.

"Why are you looking at me like that?" Carter asked. "You didn't think I was going to miss out on all the fun, did you?"

Ellery decided silence was the most prudent response but five-year-olds leaned toward honesty every time.

Bea nodded vigorously. "Uh-huh."

Carter bent down until they were eye to eye. "Someone," he said, the tease in his husky voice as new and irresistible as his smile, "has to catch Miss Ellery when she falls."

And now Ellery had another secret to keep.

The falling part?

Ellery was afraid it had already happened.

Chapter Nineteen

Carter straightened and grabbed the brooms he'd propped up against the bench. Set aside all the things cluttering up his mental to-do list in order to focus on Bea's instead.

And it felt good.

A game of broomball—a fond memory from Carter's own childhood—would feel pretty good, too.

Bea clapped her hands. "Horses!"

Carter glanced at Ellery. The tip of her nose was pink and her shoulders were shaking, but it wasn't from the cold. She could barely keep her laughter in check.

He might have rounded up the equipment to play broom hockey but Bea was obviously envisioning another kind of game.

"Horses." He repeated the word cautiously.

"Uh-huh. We have to find Snowflake. She got lost in the storm last night and doesn't know how to get home."

Carter's gaze bounced from Bea to the inn. Snowflake was a permanent fixture in the front lawn until the spring thaw.

Bea pried one of the brooms from his hand. "This one's name is Daisy 'cause it's got a yellow mane." She patted the handle and bits of mustard-colored paint sprinkled onto the ice like confetti. "Which one do you want to ride, Daddy?"

Carter turned to Ellery again. Flashed a silent request for backup.

Ellery dipped her head and Carter almost sighed in relief. Until she said, "If I were you, I would choose the red one. He looks pretty calm. Perfect for a beginner. Don't you think so, Bea?"

After a moment of contemplation, Bea nodded. "What are you going to name him?"

Name him?

Carter studied the broom. It should have been tossed in the burn pile years ago with the rest of the flotsam and jetsam that had piled up in the shed over the years. His nose twitched. "Dusty?"

Ellery muffled a coughing fit with her mitten, and Carter's eyes narrowed. She was enjoying this way too much.

"Let's go!" Bea took charge of the rescue expedition, ankles wobbling as she dragged her broom across the ice.

Carter didn't move. "I have no idea what to do."

"Use your mad investigative skills, Deputy." Ellery skated backward, using the broom for balance. "But instead of finding a missing person, you're looking for a missing horse."

"Except it's not missing," Carter pointed out. "And it's really not a horse."

Ellery smiled.

"It is to Bea."

Snow sprayed Ellery's jeans as Carter skated up to her.

They'd been on the frozen pond for over an hour. Ellery couldn't feel her toes anymore, but the warmth inside her chest had only expanded while watching Carter, former Navy SEAL and now county deputy, play cowboy.

"Jerky?"

Ellery looked down at the sticks in Carter's hand and wrinkled her nose. "No bacon?"

"Hey, lady, we're on a trail ride. You have to get used to roughing it."

"I was the one who…" Ellery's hands gripped the broom like a lifeline when she saw the now familiar black pickup truck pull up next to the barn.

Any hope that it was someone else's turn to oversee Sugar's morning routine disappeared when three doors in the cab popped open and Ellery's brothers jumped out.

"They came back, Daddy!" Bea had spotted them, too, and she waved her broom in the air.

Brendan pointed at the pond and they changed direction, taking the path Carter had shoveled to the pond instead of the one leading to the barn.

Ellery felt a stab of guilt for not telling Jameson she'd met her brothers when they'd spoken on the phone.

Until she'd been the subject of Liam's rather intense scrutiny the day before, it hadn't crossed Ellery's mind that they were observing her, too.

Spending time with her brothers would open the door for conversation and questions she couldn't answer.

Bea had followed Carter, leaving Ellery with no choice but to skate over and greet her brothers, too. They stood in a loose semi-circle at the edge of the pond, dressed in their everyday uniform of faded denim and fleece-lined jackets with the Castle Falls logo embroidered on the pocket.

"We thought we'd take Sugar for a walk and clean out the stall before Liam takes a closer look at the barn," Brendan was saying. "If that's all right with you."

Carter's brow lifted. "Do I have a choice?"

"Of course not. But it's polite to ask before we make up your mind."

Carter laughed and Ellery saw her brothers share a look. And then they looked at *her*.

"Too bad we didn't bring our skates," Brendan drawled.

"Yeah." Aiden winked at Bea. "It looks like you were having fun out there." He squatted down until they were at eye level. "What's your horse's name?"

"Daisy."

Aiden caught Carter gaping at him and grinned. "My nieces are crazy about animals. What can I say? Our canoes turn into swans or otters or dolphins, depending on the day." He gave Carter a friendly cuff on the shoulder. "So, you don't have to turn in your man card, badge or your duty belt."

"When you think about it, it's no different than the Three Musketeers running around the neighborhood with sticks while we were growing up," Liam said. "All for one…"

"One for all," Brendan and Aiden dutifully chimed in.

Ellery felt her smile slip sideways.

The Three Musketeers?

"I should get back to the house…" Ellery sank down on the bench and fumbled with the laces on her skates. Suddenly, strong, capable hands gently brushed hers aside and took over the task.

She couldn't meet Carter's eyes as he carefully untied the bows at the top and shucked off her skates.

"Thanks." Ellery sucked in a breath, unable to move when Carter's fingers curved around her ankle, holding her in place.

"Is everything okay?"

"Fine. I… I have a lot of baking to do." Ellery managed to squeeze out another smile before she started up the path, "all for one…one for all" ringing in her ears.

If her brothers' home life had been as difficult as she

thought it was, Ellery could understand their close bond. Why they'd come to rely on each other.

What she didn't understand was why they'd waited so long to find her.

"Mom?" Carter stopped dead in his tracks at the sight of Karen ensconced in the rocking chair by the window, an afghan wrapped around her shoulders like a shawl. "What are you doing down here?"

"Preventing a nervous breakdown."

The lively retort made Carter smile. "Your sense of humor is coming back, so that's a good sign."

"I think Sunni's chicken noodle soup has healing properties," Karen said. "My headache is almost gone and the only thing that hurts right now are my muscles from lying in bed for four days. I decided to make myself a cup of tea and watch a little television." A twinkle stole into her eyes. "I must admit, though, what I saw outside the window a little while ago was much more entertaining."

She nodded at the bay window, which provided an unobstructed view of the pond.

Carter hadn't blushed since middle school, but he felt one coming on.

"Bea wanted to try out her new skates."

"I really must be out of the loop," Karen said. "I didn't know you'd bought Bea an early Christmas present."

"It was Ellery…and don't get any ideas," Carter warned.

"Ideas about what?" The twinkle grew more pronounced. "It was fun to see you out there. You haven't skated on the pond since high school."

"If you ask Bea, she'll tell you we were galloping."

"Even better." Karen smiled. "I noticed Brendan and his brothers were here for quite a while."

"Liam wanted to make sure there's enough room in the

barn for the holy family, three wise men, an angel chorus, assorted shepherds and a pair of geriatric sheep I was assured will sleep through the whole thing," Carter said drily.

"I got an email from Pastor Seth this morning, thanking us for going ahead with the live nativity. It would have been almost impossible to change the location at the last minute."

"You have Ellery to thank for that. I still think providing all the food is a lot to take on."

It was possible Ellery already regretted the decision.

Carter had sensed something was wrong shortly after the Kanes arrived but he couldn't figure out what had caused the subtle change in her mood.

Ellery had claimed she was fine, but her abrupt departure said otherwise.

Carter had learned his enemies' names in the SEALS and the heavy weight pressing down on his chest was fear.

They were relying on Ellery too much. There was nothing to stop her from packing her bags and leaving the inn.

Leaving them.

"I know you need help until you're feeling better, Mom, but we should have come up with another plan."

One that would guarantee Carter would come out with his heart intact.

"I didn't ask Ellery because she knows her way around the kitchen, although I certainly don't have any doubts about her ability," Karen said. "I asked her because I see myself in her at that age."

"What do you mean?"

"I was devastated when your dad left. I was in my last month of culinary training and I'd take you with me to the test kitchen at night. Chopping onions is a great way for a woman to release all those pent-up tears."

"I don't remember any of that," Carter admitted.

"I'm not surprised. You were younger than Bea at the time. But I chopped and diced and prayed and sang silly songs with you. I leaned on God for strength…and I healed. I think Ellery is the same way. This is her first Christmas alone—"

"Alone?" The word stuck in Carter's throat as an image of some faceless man rose like a specter in his mind. "What do you mean?"

"Her parents died last spring."

"What?" The words landed like a blow. "How… When did Ellery tell you that?"

"I asked," Karen said simply. "It's so close to Christmas, I didn't want Ellery to stay here out of obligation if she had family waiting for her to come home. She didn't share any of the details, of course, but the grief is fresh. The night she arrived, I saw a young woman searching for something."

Where Ellery was concerned, Carter had only seen what he wanted to see. A modern-day princess who'd come to Castle Falls on a whim. A woman who put her needs above everyone else's.

He'd seen Jennifer.

"I can't deny that I needed Ellery's help in the kitchen, Carter," Karen said. "But I think… I think she needs us, too."

Chapter Twenty

Ellery slid another cookie sheet from the oven and set it down on an insulated pad.

Her calves ached from being on her feet all day, the scent of vanilla and cinnamon were permanently embedded in her clothing and she'd loved every minute of it.

In twenty-four hours, dozens of people would be arriving at the inn, guided by luminaries that Brendan and Aiden had placed on both sides of the driveway leading to the star shining in the peak of the barn.

Carter had taken Bea into Castle Falls to do some shopping, but Ellery's brothers had been there most of the day. She'd caught glimpses of them moving in and out of the buildings now and then. Heard the rhythmic tap of a hammer while Liam converted an empty stall into a manger, and occasional bursts of masculine laughter in the yard.

Ellery had kept her distance, afraid she wouldn't be able to hide her emotions. Which was why she'd politely declined Bea's invitation to join the family for supper, too. Carter already noticed too much.

"Can you take five, Ellery?" The man she'd successfully avoided all day poked his head into the kitchen.

Five minutes. You can handle that.

"Sure. This batch needs to cool a few minutes anyway." Ellery rinsed off her hands and wiped them on the towel looped through the tie on her apron.

She followed Carter to the living room, expecting to see the rest of the Bristow family. Karen still hadn't ventured into the kitchen, but when Ellery had brought Bea a gingerbread man to sample earlier in the day, Karen had been sitting on the couch with her laptop.

"I sent Bea and Mom upstairs to bed." Carter chuckled. "They were both falling asleep during *It's a Wonderful Life*."

"I'm glad Karen looks like herself again. In fact, I'm pretty sure she's going to boot me out of the kitchen before the guests arrive tomorrow."

"You're probably right. She also mentioned something about greeting people at the live nativity."

"Making people feel welcome is her gift."

Carter slanted a glance at her. "And speaking of gifts… I wanted your opinion on something."

Ellery tried to hide her surprise.

"While Bea was talking to Anna Leighton's twins in The Happy Cow this afternoon, I did some very last-minute Christmas shopping." Carter reached into a cabinet and pulled out a brown paper sack. "Talk about being out of your comfort zone…"

He set the contents, two small boxes, on the coffee table and motioned for Ellery to sit down.

Next to him.

Ellery sank down on the cushion and tried not to think about the fact that Carter smelled better than the cookies she'd been baking all day.

"This is for Bea." He opened the box and withdrew a delicate silver bracelet. A tiny silver horse dangled from one of the links.

Ellery recognized the charm from a display in Anna's studio.

"She's going to love it, Carter."

"Anna calls them memory charms. Mom usually does the shopping, but I wanted to get Bea something special. Something just from me."

Ellery felt tears burn the back of her eyes as Carter removed the lid from the other box.

"What do you think?"

"It's beautiful." The bracelet was similar to Bea's in design except for the tiny silver bell dangling from the chain.

"Anna said you can return it if you'd rather have something else," Carter said.

It took a moment for the words to register. And when they did...

Breathe. Ellery.

"This is for me?"

Carter nodded. "I thought you might like a memory, too."

"It's the wishing bell." The significance of the charm he'd picked out suddenly became clear. "But...you said you didn't believe that wishes can come true."

Carter smiled—he was getting really good at that—and slipped the bracelet over Ellery's wrist.

"I know. But lately I've been seeing more and more evidence that suggests otherwise."

The next morning, Ellery was wrapping the last of Bea's stocking stuffers when Karen nodded at the window.

"I think the reinforcements have arrived, Ellery." Ellery mentally prepared herself to see her brothers again and was surprised to see their significant others instead. Lily, Anna and Maddie were unloading boxes from the back of a minivan. Cassie and Chloe, Anna's twins, stood next to the vehicle, rearranging the contents of their backpacks.

"I didn't realize they were coming over today," Ellery murmured.

"Oops." Karen cringed. "That's my fault. I meant to pass along Sunni's text last night, but I was so tired I went straight to bed."

Ellery touched the bracelet peeking out from the cuff of her sweater, a reminder she hadn't dreamed that Carter had given her a gift.

The charm was a memory, he'd said. But as beautiful as the bracelet was, Ellery knew she wouldn't forget any of the moments she'd spent with Carter over the past few days.

"The volunteers will be in costume when they arrive but Rebecca Tamblin, Pastor Seth's wife, thought it would be wise to have the props here in advance," Karen went on. "That way they don't have an angel without a halo or a wise man who forgot his frankincense." Karen chuckled. "I'll walk down there and see if they need help."

"I'll go," Ellery offered quickly, afraid that Karen would overdo it if given the chance.

She grabbed her coat off the hook in the back entryway and jogged down the shoveled walkway.

"Ellery!" Lily propped a cardboard box on her hip and waved. Her lavender ski jacket paired with slim-fitting ponte leggings tucked into leather boots struck the perfect balance between UP practicality and urban chic. "We were hoping to see you."

"The guys are coming by in a little while but we wanted to see if you needed any help setting up." Maddie transferred a box to Anna and grabbed another one from the back of the van. She wore a swing coat made of gray wool and a matching cloche. "Aiden mentioned you were handling all the food prep on your own."

"But…you must have a million things to do before the wedding," Ellery protested.

"Sunni and my mom have everything under control," Anna said. "Cassie and Chloe wanted to come along and spend some time with Isabella, if that's all right."

"We brought some dolls for her to play with." One of the twins held up her backpack.

"And horses," her sister added. "Dad said those are her favorite."

Dad.

Ellery realized how little she knew about Liam and Anna's story but it was obvious Anna's twins had already embraced her brother as part of the family.

"Bea should be home any minute," she told them. "You can wait for her in the family room if you'd like."

Cassie and Chloe looked at Anna for permission and she nodded.

"Go right through the front door and Karen will show you where it is. You can grab a cookie in the dining room on your way through," Ellery told them.

"Okay!" The girls linked arms and dashed up the sidewalk.

"So, we'll unpack and organize all of this and then you can put us to work," Lily said briskly.

At the moment, Ellery felt more overwhelmed by the generous offer than the evening's event.

"I don't know what to say…"

Maddie patted Ellery's arm. "Don't say anything." Her voice dropped a notch. "When it comes to the Kane family, I've learned that it doesn't do any good."

"She's right." Lily grinned and linked her arm through Ellery's. "We girls have to stick together."

"I'm anxious to see what Liam and the guys accomplished yesterday," Maddie said.

"And meet the infamous Sugar," Anna added.

Ellery was swept along with their laughter into the barn.

The women were comfortable in any setting, it seemed, and moved in the synchronized choreography of people accustomed to working together. Ellery absorbed every bit of information she could about her brothers while they unpacked the boxes.

"Liam and Aiden were surprised Carter agreed to host the live nativity," Anna said.

"I don't think Carter had a choice." Ellery smoothed the wrinkles from a shepherd's robe. "They were very persuasive."

Maddie's fern-green eyes went wide and Lily cupped her hand over her mouth.

"What did I say?" Ellery looked from one to the other in confusion.

"It's not you." Anna was struggling to hold back her laughter. "Carter isn't the kind of guy who changes his mind unless he has a really good reason."

A smile passed around the circle and Ellery suddenly realized why.

They thought *she* was the reason.

"It's not like that." The words rushed out before Ellery could stop them. "Carter... He's been hurt. It's hard for him to trust."

"Because of Jennifer."

Ellery stared at Maddie. "You *knew* her?"

"Enough to know she was stringing Carter along. Jennifer wrote a travel blog and stopped in Castle Falls for a few weeks one summer. The number of people following her went off the charts when Carter started appearing in Jennifer's photos.

"She documented their courtship and everyone started clamoring for more. The next thing I heard, they'd gotten married on Mackinaw Island, a few weeks before Carter's deployment."

"But people don't get married for a publicity stunt," Ellery protested.

"It depends on the kind of person they are," Maddie said. "Jennifer was beautiful and ambitious and I think she was willing to do anything it took to rise to the top.

"No one really knows what happened after that. Jennifer moved back to Chicago while Carter was serving overseas. I'm guessing when family life became a liability instead of an asset, she wanted a divorce."

"Wow." Lily breathed the word. "I think I'd have a hard time trusting anyone after that, too, but you can't give up on Carter, Ellery. We've all witnessed the amazing things God can do in a person's life."

"Witnessed *and* experienced," Anna added candidly. "I wasn't very trusting when I met Liam. Ross, my first husband, was abusive. I couldn't see myself ever marrying again."

"And Maddie turned Aiden down when he asked her on a date." Lily smiled at her friend. "She was the only one who couldn't see they were perfect for each other."

"It's true. When Aiden asked for my help with some research, I tried to convince myself he was no different from anyone else who came into the library. I had a lot of fears and insecurities and the thought of falling in love was as terrifying as bungee jumping off Eagle Rock."

"I'm not in *love* with Carter," Ellery choked out. "I barely know him."

The three women exchanged another smile.

"But sometimes," Anna said softly, "you just know."

Carter knew he was in trouble when the Kane brothers cornered him behind the woodpile.

"You're going to have to find a better hiding spot next time," Aiden said. "We're professionals."

"I wasn't…" Carter stopped. Because he kind of *was*. But not from them. From himself. His feelings.

Ellery.

Because she was getting under his skin. Big-time.

"I thought you were in the barn, getting things ready for tonight."

"We're finished." Brendan bent down and started tossing pieces of kindling into the bin.

"What are you doing?"

"Moving this project along." Liam yanked the ax from the chopping block. "Your mom invited us in for a cup of hot chocolate and many hands make light work, right?"

No one waited for Carter to answer. In twenty minutes, his "unit" had chopped and stacked enough firewood to last until the new year.

The women had already shed their outerwear and were clustered around the fireplace in the gathering room, drawing from its warmth.

And inevitably, Carter's gaze was drawn to Ellery.

For a woman who'd willingly spent the last few days preparing for a community-wide event, the guarded smile on Ellery's face looked out of place.

He couldn't imagine Lily, Anna and Maddie were to blame. All three had a reputation for welcoming people into the community. Which left…him.

For the hundredth time that day, Carter questioned his decision to give Ellery the charm bracelet.

Now who was guilty of overstepping?

Carter realized he'd been caught staring when Aiden's elbow dug into his ribs.

"Hello? If I stopped in the middle of traffic like that I'd get a parking ticket."

"You might get one anyway," Carter growled. "I know your license plate number."

Aiden wasn't listening. He'd loped over to Maddie's side and wrapped his arm around her slender waist. "Hey, beautiful."

Maddie, sweet, introverted librarian that she was, rolled her eyes. "Your ancestors might have been able to get away with blarney like that, Aiden Kane, but I'm completely immune to your charm."

Her wide smile said otherwise.

Karen swept into the room with a tray of cookies and Carter was relieved to see her energy had returned.

"Here you go!" she sang out. "The girls are having a tea party in the living room, so I served them first, but there's a hot chocolate station and more snacks in the dining room."

Lily had drifted over to Brendan's side and he looked as smitten as his brothers when she tucked her arm through his. "Thank you, Karen."

"I'm the one who should be thanking all of you." Karen set the tray on the coffee table. "The wedding is in less than forty-eight hours and you gave up an entire afternoon to help with the nativity."

Carter felt a sudden shift in the climate of the room.

Liam stepped closer to Anna and reached for her hand. "Sunni and Nancy have everything under control."

"I've no doubt they do!" Karen tossed a smile over her shoulder when she reached the door. "I'm going to peek in on the girls, but I expect everyone to have a plate and a cup of hot chocolate in their hands when I get back."

No one moved.

"Aiden—" Brendan reached out his hand but Aiden shook his head. With a murmured "Excuse me," he strode out of the room, leaving an awkward silence in his wake.

Anna turned her face into Liam's shoulder and released a quiet sigh.

Carter frowned. He'd seen Aiden interact on numerous occasions with his future sister-in-law and hadn't picked up on any strain in the relationship. It seemed impossible he disapproved of Liam's upcoming marriage but a quick glance at Ellery told Carter the same troubling thought had occurred to her, as well.

"Aiden is thrilled our family is expanding," Lily said, almost as if she'd read their minds. She glanced at Brendan, a question in her eyes and he, in turn, looked at Liam.

"But he's upset because we're still missing one," Liam said slowly.

"One what?" Carter asked.

"Member of the family." Liam drew Anna into the circle of his arms. "It's common knowledge around Castle Falls that we were in a bad situation before Sunni and Rich took us in. Carla, our biological mom, didn't exactly keep it a secret that she wished she'd never had us. What she didn't tell us was that we had—*have*—a sister."

Carter heard Ellery pull in a breath and realized she was as stunned as he was by Liam's quiet admission.

"I overheard a conversation between Carla and someone from the adoption agency when I skipped school one day," Brendan said. "I assumed she'd hidden her pregnancy from everyone and given the baby up for adoption after it was born. Liam and Aiden...they'd gone through enough, so I didn't tell them until last summer."

"You were just a child yourself and you were protecting your brothers." Lily's voice was gentle but firm, evidence they'd had this discussion before. "By not changing your last name to Mason after Sunni adopted you, you left a door open for her to find you, too."

"I waited too long." Guilt flashed in Brendan's eyes. "If it hadn't been for me, we could have found her years ago."

"Lily is right, Bren. You can't beat yourself up," Liam told him. "Anna can attest to the fact that when you told us about our sister, the first emotion I felt was relief. I wouldn't have wanted her to go through what we did as kids. Aiden was the one who moved forward. He convinced Maddie to help him find her before the wedding."

"Aiden didn't have a lot to go on, though. It was a closed adoption with a private agency and we didn't know her birthday or even her name…" Brendan's voice thickened. "Maddie was able to track down Carla's best friend and found out more details.

"Apparently our sister had some medical problems when she was born and ended up in the NICU for several months. A woman who volunteered at the hospital spent a lot of time with her and somehow convinced Carla to grant her and her husband temporary guardianship. It wasn't supposed to be a permanent situation but the couple ended up adopting her instead."

Brendan paused and glanced at Liam, almost as if he were hesitant to continue the story.

"And this is where the story begins to sound like one of those made-for-television movies," Liam said. "We assumed Carla had terminated her parental rights right away, but the adoption wasn't finalized until our sister was five years old."

Carter heard the tension flowing through Liam's voice. "I'm guessing there's some significance in that?"

"Oh, yeah." Brendan and Liam tossed another look back and forth. "Aiden was five years old at the time, too."

Before Carter's brain finished connecting the dots, Aiden appeared in the doorway.

"My sister and I…we're twins."

Chapter Twenty-One

Twins.

Ellery stared at Aiden with new eyes as her mind struggled to process everything she'd just heard.

Her throat tightened. And tightened. Until barely a whisper of air could get through.

She was the "research" Maddie had mentioned? The reason the couple was together?

"I'm sorry." Aiden made a beeline for Maddie's side again. "I had to take a few minutes…get my head on straight again and remember that God's timing is perfect."

Brendan's expression softened. "We all need to remember that."

"The agency won't turn over her records?" Carter asked.

"We wrote a letter explaining the situation but they wouldn't budge. Some hotshot attorney sent us a letter saying that our sister was out of the country and they'd make a *recommendation*—" Aiden put air quotes around the word "—based on the information, but that was weeks ago. We might have to accept the fact she doesn't want anything to do with us."

Ellery flinched at the pain in his voice.

"Don't give up yet. You have no idea what's going on behind the scenes."

Ellery felt another internal shock wave and blindly reached for the back of the closest chair.

Carter. Encouraging Aiden to…to *hope.*

"I know," Aiden said. "But like your mom said, the wedding is less than forty-eight hours away and we really wanted her to be there…" His voice trailed off as Anna's twins rushed in, their laughter chasing the shadows from the room.

"Something's wrong." Aiden rubbed his eyes and pretended to blink. "I'm seeing double."

"You always say that, Uncle Aiden!" One of the girls said.

"How am I supposed to tell you two apart when you always dress alike?"

"We didn't *try* to pick out the same outfit." Chloe looked at her sister's matching sweatshirt and jeans. "It just happens."

"Don't bother trying to figure it out," Liam said with a laugh. "I've been told it's a 'twin thing.'"

"Miss Karen says it's time for hot chocolate," Cassie announced.

Aiden tipped his head to one side. "If hot chocolate gets cold, then what do you call it?" he mused.

The twins erupted into giggles and a fissure of grief opened up inside of Ellery.

Her parents had to have known about Aiden when they'd adopted her. If what her brothers had said about their home life was true, shouldn't they have intervened on his behalf, too?

Tears scorched Ellery's eyes as she walked down the hall. Carter fell into step beside her. She felt, rather than saw, his sideways glance.

"That was quite a story."

Ellery managed a nod. What she really wanted to do was step into Carter's arms, rest her head against the solid warmth of his chest and tell him it was her story, too.

Ellery just didn't know how—or when—she could fill in the missing pieces.

Brendan had said he'd waited too long to find her, but when it came right down to it, wasn't she guilty of the same thing?

Would her brothers understand why she'd kept her identity a secret? Would they forgive her for having doubts of her own?

God, I know I made a promise to Jameson, but I can't put my brothers through any more pain. Aiden said he trusts Your timing and I will, too. Please give me an opportunity to tell them the truth.

Bea had gotten there ahead of everyone else and was helping her grandmother add more snacks to the already generous buffet.

Ellery's stomach felt like one gigantic knot but she grabbed a ceramic mug decorated with sprigs of holly and reached for the carafe of hot chocolate and filled her cup. Turned and almost ran into Liam.

"Wow." He was looking down at Ellery's cup with a blend of amusement and disbelief.

"Is something wrong?"

"No." A smile rustled at the corners of Liam's lips. "There's only one other person I know who sprinkles popcorn on their hot chocolate instead of marshmallows."

He pointed at Aiden's mug and Ellery saw a layer of popcorn bobbing on the surface of the hot chocolate.

They'd been raised in different homes. Led completely different lives. And yet they had this crazy, quirky little thing in common.

Ellery felt an inner nudge and drew in a shaky breath. Smiled at Aiden.

"It must be a twin thing."

Carter tensed at Ellery's side and Brendan took a step forward. Stopped.

"Ellery." He stared at her as if the scales had dropped from his eyes. "You. You're…"

Ellery swallowed hard and nodded.

"There were reasons I didn't tell you." Reasons that seemed ridiculous now.

The three little girls picked up on the tension swirling in the air and fell silent.

"You know what this means, don't you?" Aiden's voice sounded husky.

Ellery shook her head.

"I can't claim the title as the best-looking one in the family anymore."

Ellery's laugh turned into a sob as her brothers surged forward and embraced her.

Carter swung the ax and bisected the piece of oak centered on the chopping block. Picked up the shards of kindling and tossed them onto the growing pile.

A scrap of colorful paper cartwheeled across the snow, a colorful remnant from the live nativity that had somehow escaped the cleanup crew.

Gunmetal clouds moved sluggishly across the sky, their dark underbellies weighted down with snow, but Carter couldn't blame the bone-deep numbness that had spread throughout his body on the falling temperature.

No. He blamed Ellery.

He'd had no idea the Kane brothers had been searching for a missing sister, but to find out that sister was Ellery…

Everyone in the room had looked as if Christmas had

come early, but Carter felt as if they'd skipped right to April Fool's Day.

And guess who was the fool?

Carter's gut churned as scenes began to unfold in his memory.

Ellery's reluctance to talk about her personal life. The questions she'd asked about the Kane family when they were together.

Carter was *trained* to be observant. To see things other people missed. And yet he'd totally missed the fact that Ellery had used him to gather intel on her brothers.

"Can we talk?"

He froze at the sound of Ellery's voice behind him.

She'd been protected by a six-foot-tall wall of men at the live nativity and left the inn just after dawn. Carter knew what time it was because he'd been awake most of the night.

After the bombshell she'd dropped, Carter wasn't surprised Ellery had gone over to Sunni Mason's house, but he'd caught Bea staring out the window at least a dozen times over the course of the day, waiting for her return.

Carter set another log on the block and Ellery stopped a few feet away. The sight of her red-rimmed eyes and tremulous smile told a story, too, but Carter refused to be taken in again.

"I'd say you had plenty of opportunities to do that over the past two weeks."

"I know. And I'm sorry." Ellery tucked her hands into the pockets of the thin leather coat she'd been wearing the day they met. "I promised Jameson—my attorney—I wouldn't tell anyone who I was."

Ellery kept an attorney on retainer.

The chasm between them widened.

"And who is that, exactly?" Carter asked, unable to

keep the bitterness from leaking into his voice. "Is Ellery Marshall your real name? Or did you lie about that, too?"

Ellery flinched. "I didn't lie about anything. My parents never told me anything about my family history or that I had siblings. When the agency contacted Jameson and said my brothers wanted to meet me, he was concerned about their motives. He thought it was suspicious they'd waited until after my parents passed away to reach out to me. Jameson wanted to hire a private investigator to do some digging, but I couldn't wait. I... I didn't want to read about my brothers in a report."

Every softly spoken word ripped out a piece of Carter's heart.

"I guess it was pretty convenient you ended up here, then, wasn't it?"

Confusion flickered in her eyes. "What do you mean?"

"It was the perfect place for a recon mission. We needed help, and it gave you an excuse to stay longer."

"It wasn't like that." Ellery was staring at him as if he were a stranger.

Well, now she knew what it felt like.

"No? You didn't pump me for information about the Kanes whenever we were together? The questions you asked about Aiden's accident, about their business, wasn't an attempt to find out if they are struggling financially and need a helping hand?"

Ellery opened her mouth to deny it but Carter had already seen the truth flash across her face.

"You can understand why I had doubts, too. My parents insisted on a closed adoption to protect me and I always trusted their judgment. I wanted to make sure my brothers wanted *me*, not the things I could do for them."

Carter understood why Ellery's adoptive parents had wanted to protect their daughter.

Something he'd failed to do. Again.

He should have known better than to let Bea spend time with Ellery.

"I could have told you everything you wanted to know about the Kanes the day you arrived, you know." Carter gave voice to one of the thoughts that had taunted him during the night. "But I guess it doesn't matter because the end result is the same. You got what you wanted."

"Carter—"

"Are we done here?" He tried to ignore the tear that washed over the breaker of sable lashes and cut a crooked path down Ellery's cheek. "It's Christmas Eve, and I have things to do."

"Yes, I should have confided in you. And although you don't believe me, I stayed because... Karen needed help, not to gather more information about my brothers."

A heartbeat of silence followed as she waited for Carter to say something.

When he didn't, she nodded and walked away, taking what was left of Carter's heart with her.

Liam and Anna's wedding didn't officially start for another half hour, but Ellery saw guests already filing into the building when she pulled into the parking lot of New Life Fellowship.

The church her brothers attended was tucked in a grove of birch trees at the edge of a quiet residential street in Castle Falls. Like the other buildings in town, the brick exterior had been mellowed by time and the elements. A rustic cross rose from the top of the steeple and stained-glass panels framed each of the windows.

Several people paused to glance in Ellery's direction as she got out of the car. Her hands began to shake and she pushed them into the pockets of her faux-fur jacket.

Ellery should have been more specific when she'd called Philomena and asked her to overnight an outfit suitable for a winter wedding. Wrapped in tissue paper was the dress Ellery had worn to a charity gala the year before. Made from yards of ice-blue velvet, the full skirt landed an inch above the knees and dozens of tiny crystal beads shimmered on the bodice.

Phil, who was as skilled at putting together a wardrobe as she was a dinner party, believed in a woman having the proper accessories, too. She'd added three pairs of shoes for Ellery to choose from and a tiny jeweled clutch.

But it was the slender box from Tiffany's that jump-started a fresh round of tears.

She'd lifted the necklace from its bed of satin and traced her finger over the five pearls threaded on a delicate gold chain.

Five.

According to Candace, they'd bought the necklace in honor of Ellery's first birthday and placed it in safekeeping until she was older. Ellery hadn't understood the significance behind the number of pearls until now. Her parents had been celebrating her first birthday with *them.*

"Ellery?"

Ellery realized she'd reached the door. The red-haired woman holding it open was the same one she'd met at The Happy Cow the day she'd brought Bea there for ice cream.

"Yes."

"I'm Nancy Leighton, Anna's mother. I was told to watch for you." Ellery was guided into a spacious entry-way.

Tall, freestanding candelabras wrapped in ivory tulle flanked the doors to the sanctuary but Nancy pointed to a hallway branching off from the main entryway. "It's the second door on your right."

Ellery didn't have time to ask questions. Anna's mother was already bustling away.

The door was closed but Ellery could hear laughter on the other side. Before she could knock, it swung open and Ellery was yanked inside. Enveloped in an effusive hug and a cloud of perfume.

"You're just in time!"

She found herself looking into Sunni Mason's warm brown eyes.

After spending the day with her brothers' adoptive mom, Ellery knew why their loyalty ran so deep. Sunni and Candace had a lot in common and Ellery had no doubt, if the two women had ever met, they would have become good friends.

Ellery was swept into a flurry of activity. Lily and Maddie, beautiful in emerald green organza, were in the process of weaving satin ribbons into Cassie's and Chloe's braids. The twins' matching dresses were the same color as the bridesmaids' but the skirts were made of heavy tulle and belled out around their ankles.

Anna emerged from behind a three-paneled screen and the hum of conversation stopped as every pair of eyes turned toward the bride.

Anna's wedding gown was beautiful in its simplicity. Ivory satin the perfect complement to her chestnut hair and unusual amber eyes. Eyes that looked a little apprehensive now.

"Well? Will someone please say something?"

"Wow." Cassie broke the silence and everyone laughed.

"I think that word sums it up," Sunni said. "I'll be surprised if Liam doesn't fall over in a dead faint when he sees you coming down the aisle."

"You'll need this." Lily handed her future sister-in-law

a bouquet made up of peonies and white roses. "Now, what are we missing?"

"Your shoes are fresh from the box, so we've got the 'something new' covered." Maddie tucked a lace handkerchief into the center of Anna's flowers. "And this is your 'something old.'"

"So, that means you have to borrow something from one of us."

Ellery was already unfastening the clasp on her necklace. "You can wear these."

Anna's eyes went wide. "Oh, Ellery...your pearls. They're beautiful, but I can't..."

"Please," Ellery said. "I'd like to contribute something to the wedding."

"Your being here today is all we need," Lily said.

Tears banked in Ellery's eyes and Maddie immediately began to dole out more handkerchiefs.

"Why is everyone crying?" Cassie asked in a low voice.

"I think they're happy tears," her twin whispered back.

"Chloe is right, but even happy tears can make a girl's mascara run." Sunni grinned at Maddie. "You better restock those tissues while I check on the men. It's almost time."

Her words sparked another flurry of activity and Ellery slipped quietly from the room.

Thank You, God. Being here today...watching Anna and Liam exchange their vows... It was so much more than I expected.

Ellery felt another attack of nerves as she retraced her steps down the hallway, even though the chances of Carter attending the wedding were about the same as him forgiving her for not telling him the truth right away.

Based on what she'd learned about his past, Ellery

should have anticipated Carter's reaction. He thought she'd used him, manipulated him the way Jennifer had.

Yes, she'd come to Castle Falls to find her brothers. But she'd stayed to help Karen. And…because of him.

A teenage boy with short, sandy-brown hair and wire-framed glasses offered Ellery his arm at the door leading into the sanctuary.

Anna and Liam had chosen to have a small wedding, but Ellery could feel the furtive looks from close friends and family as the teen escorted her down the aisle. She paused when they reached the center of the room and slipped her arm free.

"This is fine. Thank you."

The boy looked confused. "Aren't you Ellery Marshall?"

"Yes."

"Liam said I'm supposed to escort you to the first row. The one reserved for family."

Ellery couldn't hear the piano over the rushing sound in her ears as she took her seat. She would have been content to remain on the sidelines today. Being able to attend Liam and Anna's wedding was enough, but the family made her feel as if she belonged.

A low murmur swept through the church as the men filed in behind Pastor Tamblin. Her brothers had exchanged their usual flannel and denim for charcoal-gray tuxedoes. Wind-tossed hair was tamed, faces clean-shaven. They looked like strangers again. Until Aiden caught Ellery's eye and winked.

Ellery winked back.

Pastor Tamblin opened in prayer and the pianist began to play the processional.

Lily and Maddie walked down the aisle in single file

and both of them smiled at Ellery before they took their places at the front of the sanctuary.

The music changed and Anna appeared. Ellery had assumed Cassie and Chloe would act as flower girls, but when they each took hold of one of Anna's hands, it became clear the twins were escorting their mother down the aisle.

Ellery fumbled for a tissue and saw a dozen other people do the same as everyone rose to their feet to honor the bride.

Her heart felt incredibly full as she watched Liam bend down and give the twins a hug.

This was a family who made room. Brokenness had made them bigger, allowing God's light to shine through.

She and her brothers had talked for hours the previous day, taking turns sharing their stories, and Ellery had silently thanked God that her brothers had had each other. Thanked Him that Sunni and Rich Mason had opened up their hearts and their home.

There was so much she'd missed, growing up without them, but there'd been wonderful gifts along the way. Ellery had had parents who'd loved and encouraged her. Taught her about a God who kept His promises.

Ellery couldn't change the past even if she wanted to, but she trusted God with her future.

Even if that future didn't include Carter.

Chapter Twenty-Two

Carter peeled off his coat and hung it on the hook in the back hallway.

He hadn't planned to spend the majority of the day on Christmas Eve trudging through the woods, trying to locate a teenage girl who'd been injured while cross-country skiing, but he couldn't ignore someone who needed help even when he wasn't technically on call.

He'd heard the chatter on the radio and knew the deputies on duty were clear across the county, having responded to an accident scene. Carter had quickly changed into his uniform and driven to the trailhead, where the teen's terrified twelve-year-old sister had hiked out alone and dialed 911. To complicate matters, the girl couldn't pinpoint her sister's exact location on the map because they'd veered off the marked trail.

The girls' parents and the county K-9 unit were en route, but waiting wasn't an option when a light snow continued to fall, covering the girls' tracks. He'd instructed the younger sister to wait in the squad car, where she could stay connected to dispatch until her parents arrived.

Then Carter had struck out into the woods with his

medical bag and an inner peace that told him he wasn't alone.

"Carter." Karen padded into the hallway, wearing her robe and slippers. She searched his face and expelled a sigh of relief. "You found her."

Carter nodded. "A fractured ankle, some bruised ribs and a touch of hypothermia, but she should be fine."

"Praise God," Karen murmured. "I've been praying."

Carter had, too. When he'd spotted the girl curled up in a ball at the bottom of the ridge, injured but alive. When the darkness had swallowed everything but the beam of Carter's flashlight as he'd carried her the half mile back to the squad car.

It had felt right, leaning into God, leaning on His strength, instead of relying solely on his own.

And when the teen was reunited with her family, Carter's silent prayer of gratitude felt like another step in the right direction, too.

Karen linked her arm through his. "You're probably starving. I kept the soup and the coffee hot for you."

"Bea's asleep?"

"It's been a busy few days."

Busy didn't begin to describe it, Carter thought.

"Carter..." Karen fiddled with a terry-cloth belt tied around her waist. "Ellery checked out before she went to Liam and Anna's wedding this evening."

The floor shifted underneath Carter's feet. "She *left*?"

"Sunni invited her to stay at the house for a few days."

She'd left. On Christmas Eve.

"Does Bea know?"

Karen nodded. "She helped Ellery pack up her things. Ellery promised she'd be back, which made it a little easier, I think."

Coming back to say goodbye.

But what did he expect? He'd practically chased her away.

Carter opened Bea's door and quietly entered the room. She was sound asleep, one arm tucked underneath her pillow, the other holding tight to one of her many treasures.

Carter eased it from her grip. On the cover was a stick figure with bright blue eyes and a smile that extended from one yellow pigtail to another. He read the words neatly printed across the top. *Isabella's Best Christmas Ever.*

This was the book Ellery had told him about.

Carter sank into the rocking chair and his fingers shook a little as he turned the pages.

Bea knew what mattered most…and so did Ellery.

She was the one who'd encouraged him to be present, to make memories with his daughter, when she'd been dealing with a terrible loss of her own.

Every good and perfect gift is from above, and cometh down from the Father of Lights, with whom there is no variableness, neither shadow of turning.

The verse Pastor Seth had quoted during his message at the live nativity flashed through Carter's mind.

God had given Carter gifts he'd been too afraid to open.

He'd done a little investigating of his own. Convinced himself that Ellery was a woman who had everything. Financial security. A fulfilling career. And now a family.

Why would she need him?

His dad had left. Jennifer had left. Leaving Carter with a gaping wound. A reminder he wasn't enough.

And walking that shadowy path instead of letting God light the way, he'd come to the conclusion that God had abandoned him, too.

God, I messed up. You've been here all along but I didn't see it. I don't know what You've got planned, but I'm in, no matter what. I'll make mistakes but Ellery was right. Those are better than regrets.

"Daddy?" Bea was sitting up in bed.

"Hey, Issybea."

"Is it Christmas?"

"Almost."

Bea reached out her arms and Carter sat down on the edge of the bed. She snuggled against his chest and her gaze dropped to the book in his hand.

"That's my book, Daddy. I drew the cover myself."

Carter cleared his throat. "You did a great job."

"Can you read it again?"

"Sure."

Somehow, he made it through a second time.

"There's one more." Bea turned the book over. On the back, three stick figures, one a woman with sable-brown hair and vivid, blue-green eyes.

Ellery.

"Uh-huh. But I couldn't finish it," Bea said. "'Cause I don't know how to spell all the words."

Carter snagged one of the crayons scattered on Bea's nightstand. "Maybe Daddy can help you with that. What do you want to say?"

"Miss El'ry stays forever."

Carter's arms tightened around his daughter.

That was what he wanted, too.

Ellery winced when the floorboards creaked underneath her feet.

The house was quiet, but she'd been awake for hours, staring up the ceiling in Sunni Mason's guest room. She'd finally given up on sleep and gone downstairs in search of a cup of coffee. Her solitary wanderings led her to the room behind the kitchen, where a wall of windows framed a stunning view of the river.

All the evidence of Liam and Anna's wedding reception had been swept away, but hundreds of tiny white lights winked in the branches of the Christmas tree and a row of hand-knit stockings bulging with treasure hung from the fireplace mantel. The family had unanimously voted to delay the official gift opening until Anna and Liam returned from a short honeymoon, but Sunni must have decided the twins needed some small gifts to tide them over.

"There's one for you, too."

Ellery turned and saw Brendan standing a few feet behind her. "I haven't had a stocking for years."

"It's a Kane family tradition…" Brendan closed his eyes. "I'm sorry, Ellery."

"You don't have to be." Ellery smiled. "It was thoughtful of Sunni to include me."

Brendan didn't smile back. "I wasn't talking about the stockings. I'm sorry I didn't tell Aiden and Liam about you sooner. We could have been there for you when you lost your parents, but instead you had to face everything alone." A muscle worked in his jaw. "I was afraid that if Aiden didn't find you, he'd never forgive me. Now I'm hoping you can."

"Brendan…no." Ellery closed the distance between them, reached out and squeezed her big brother's hand. "It was because of my parents that I know I *wasn't* alone. I was driving myself crazy, wondering why they didn't share any details about my biological family, but I know it was because they were protecting me. Just like you were protecting Liam and Aiden.

"We've missed out on a lot of years, but I believe God brought us back together again at *exactly* the right time."

Brendan's sigh of relief left a smile in its wake. "That's what Aiden said, but don't you dare tell him I said so."

He plucked a foil-wrapped Santa from the stocking with Aiden's name embroidered on it. "Or that I gave you this."

"I heard my name. And quit trying to bribe Ellery with chocolate." Aiden sauntered into the room, Dodger tripping along at his heels. "I'm already her favorite."

Brendan rolled his eyes. "You think you're everyone's favorite."

Ellery grinned.

"Can I help it that people are drawn to my rapier wit and exceptional good looks?" Aiden winked at Ellery. "Merry Christmas, sis."

"Merry Christmas."

Sis.

Sweeter than the chocolate Santa.

Dodger peeled away from Aiden's side and trotted over to Ellery. He dropped at her feet, tail wagging.

"Shameless groveling," Aiden muttered as Ellery bent down to scratch the dog's ears.

Scars bisected the fur on Dodger's back like the seams on a patchwork quilt, visual remnants of the trauma he'd experienced. Carter had downplayed his role in the dog's rescue and recovery, but he was the reason Dodger had found a forever home with her brother.

Carter was a good man, too. And it wasn't because he'd adhered to a code of honor in the SEALS or followed his training as an officer. It was because he cared.

That was the man Ellery had fallen in love with.

Sometimes you just know, Lily had said.

But Carter wasn't ready to put the past behind him and love her back.

Ellery had been concerned about her brothers' reaction when she'd told them the truth. It hadn't occurred to her that Carter was the one who would feel betrayed.

Aiden filched a candy cane from Liam's stocking. "He'll

never miss it. It's a good thing candy canes are in season. We bought them in bulk after we found out they were Sugar's weakness."

"That little girl is going to be pretty excited when she sees the big red bow on Sugar's stall this morning," Brendan said.

"Bow?" Ellery echoed.

"Carter called Sunni a few days ago and said they wanted to keep her." Her brother shook his head. "I have no idea what got into him. Maybe he watched *A Christmas Carol*."

Or read a book.

Ellery wished she could see Bea's face when she realized Sugar's forever home would be with her.

Tomorrow's Christmas, El'ry. Aren't you going to be here when I open my presents?

The question had torn Ellery up inside. Unlike her father, Bea thought Ellery belonged with them.

"Ellery?" Brendan sounded so serious that Ellery felt a stab of alarm. "I know the last forty-eight hours have been a little crazy, but there's something we'd like you to think about.

"We know you have responsibilities in Grand Rapids, but Liam and Anna would love to spend more time with you when they get back from their honeymoon and we're feeling kind of selfish where you're concerned…"

"What Bren is trying to say is that we want you to stay a few weeks," Aiden cut in. "Dodge and I will camp out in my old room and you can have the apartment above the garage. It's set with Wi-Fi, so you can work remotely if there are deadlines to make for the foundation."

Tears welled up in Ellery's eyes. "I would love to spend more time with you but I need to go back to Grand Rapids for a few days…" She held up her hand when it looked like her brothers were going to protest. "I have to talk to Jameson in person." She tempered the words with a smile. "Shop for fleece and insulated boots."

And put some distance between her and Carter so her heart could begin to heal.

Chapter Twenty-Three

Carter stood on the front steps of Sunni Mason's home, Bea's book in his coat pocket and wearing a Santa hat made from construction paper, because facing Ellery wasn't difficult enough.

The door swung open before he could knock. Aiden and Brendan blocked the doorway. Carter took one look at their faces and realized he was going to have to use all his negotiation tactics to get past them. It was too bad that Liam, the most reasonable of the three brothers, had left for his honeymoon.

"I'm here to see Ellery."

Brendan folded his arms across his chest. "And you think she wants to see you?"

"Probably not," Carter admitted.

"This is the first Christmas we've spent with our sister. Come back tomorrow."

That was too easy. Carter's eyes narrowed. "Will Ellery be here tomorrow?"

Their disgruntled expressions answered the question.

"I really need to talk to her."

"Why?" Aiden folded his arms over his chest. "Did you remember a few more things she did wrong?"

Carter deserved that. "It wasn't Ellery. I was the one who messed up. I was…"

"Out of line?" Brendan supplied.

"Stupid?" Aiden tossed another one into the mix.

"Both."

Aiden nudged Brendan. "Sidebar."

They stepped to one side and turned their backs on Carter.

"…been hurt enough," he heard Brendan mutter.

It occurred to Carter that a future with Ellery wasn't the only thing he'd put in jeopardy. There was a very real possibility he'd lost the friendship of men he'd come to respect and admire.

While Carter was weighing the odds of making it past them without being tackled, they blocked his path again, their expressions grim.

"We've been in your shoes," Brendan said, stunning Carter down to his boots. "And we got a second chance to get it right."

"Thanks—"

"Just don't blow it," Aiden warned.

Hope, the elusive thing Carter had once dismissed as a weakness, gave him the courage to walk through the door, Santa hat and all.

He followed Brendan and Aiden as they sauntered down the hallway and ushered him into a spacious family room.

Carter took one look at the mountain of discarded wrapping paper and realized he'd interrupted the family's Christmas.

Anna's twins were sprawled on the rug playing a board game. Maddie Montgomery was perched in a wingback chair, sipping hot chocolate, while Brendan's wife, Lily, tried to wrestle a ribbon from the jaws of an overweight basset hound.

Sunni was the first one to realize her sons weren't alone.

Their eyes met across the room and she nodded, almost as if she'd been expecting him.

Huh.

Carter took a tentative step toward Ellery. She sat on a braided rug in front of the fireplace, Dodger draped over her legs as she watched the twins.

For a moment, Carter simply drank in the sight of her. Her feet were bare and a baggy gray sweatshirt with the Castle Falls logo silk-screened on the front brushed the knees of her faded jeans.

The speech Carter had rehearsed on the drive to Castle Falls Outfitters dissolved like water on a hot griddle as her head turned in his direction.

Sunni clapped her hands, breaking the silence that had fallen over the room. "Okay, everyone. It's time to start brunch, and I could use a little help in the kitchen."

Everyone filed through the door and Carter had no doubt Ellery would exit the room right along with them if he didn't give her a reason to stay.

"Ellery… I really need to talk to you."

The wary look on her beautiful face just about wrecked him. He'd stepped away instead of stepping up, and Ellery had mistaken his silence as rejection.

The irony of that wasn't lost on Carter. He'd been afraid she was going to reject *him*.

"Okay." Ellery crossed her arms, waiting for him to explain.

"I…" The glimpse of a tiny silver bell dangling from the bracelet on her wrist momentarily robbed Carter of the ability to speak.

Worry flashed in Ellery's eyes. "Is everything all right at home?"

No. It wasn't. Not even close. Because she wasn't there.

"Carter?" Ellery pressed when he didn't answer. "Is it your mom? B-Bea?"

Carter shouldn't have been surprised that Ellery was concerned about his family. That he'd thought for even a moment that this woman was as self-absorbed and manipulative as Jennifer was more proof of his stupidity.

He'd been running. From God. From himself. So focused on not repeating past mistakes he'd pushed away the only woman he could imagine a future with.

"Bea is fine...or at least she will be. She asked me to deliver a Christmas gift."

Now Carter's unexpected visit made sense. He would do anything for Bea.

But for one crazy moment, when Ellery had seen Carter walked into the living room with her brothers, she'd thought he'd had a change of heart.

Carter dipped his hand into the pocket of his coat and pulled out a package wrapped in gold foil. "You have to open it now."

Ellery didn't know how long she could hold her smile in place, but she'd do anything for Bea, too. Carter watched her fumble with the tape and peel back the paper.

She stared down at the cover of a very familiar book.

"I can't accept this," Ellery protested. "Bea wrote it for you."

"Apparently, it wasn't finished." Carter's hand closed over Ellery's when she tried to give it back to him. "She added something else last night."

Ellery was acutely aware of Carter's gaze as she flipped through the pages until she reached the end of the book. "I don't see..."

"Back cover."

Ellery stifled a wild urge to laugh.

Carter couldn't have *led* with that?

Ellery turned the book over and stole the breath from her lungs. Because the stick-figure woman in the center of the picture, the one holding Bea's and Carter's hands, had short, dark brown hair and blue-green eyes.

"She asked me to deliver the message that goes with it, too." Carter's husky voice tugged against nerve endings already stretched thin from the events of the past few days. "Would you like to hear it?"

Ellery couldn't look at Carter. Couldn't move without dislodging the tears that had banked in her eyes.

Fortunately, Carter didn't wait for Ellery's permission.

"Miss El'ry stays forever."

God, this is too hard.

A tear broke free and zigzagged down Ellery's cheek. She lifted her hand to wipe it away, but Carter beat her to it. Instead of staunching the flow, the gentleness of his touch threatened to open the floodgates even more.

"Tell her…thank you." Ellery pivoted blindly toward the door, but Carter was suddenly in front of her.

"Ellery? It's what I want, too."

No. She couldn't have heard… Ellery's own tears were forgotten when she saw the diamond-bright sheen in Carter's eyes.

"Yesterday, I was afraid of making a mistake, but the biggest mistake would be letting you walk out of my life without telling you how I feel." Carter paused, as if struggling to find the right words. "After Jennifer left, I convinced myself that I could live without love…but I can't live without you, Ellery. I don't *want* to live without you. You turn scarves into reins and brooms into horses and you…you focus on the light instead of the shadows. You're the one who taught me to smile again." A corner of his lips inched up. "Literally."

The lump in Ellery's throat made it difficult to speak. Carter must have misinterpreted her silence for hesitation, because he took a step backward, his hands fisted at his sides.

"After the way I treated you, I don't deserve your forgiveness, let alone a second chance…"

Love welled up inside of Ellery. She released a slow breath. Extended her hand.

"Ellery Marshall. I'm twenty-five years old and I run a nonprofit called the Marshall Foundation. I love puttering in the kitchen and ice-skating and sleigh rides and spending time with the people I love. I live in Grand Rapids, but I'm considering making Castle Falls my permanent home."

Carter looked confused for a moment and then his smile expanded into that heart-stopping, take-no-prisoners grin.

"It's nice to meet you." He shook her hand and Ellery took a risk of her own. Instead of letting go, she stepped into the circle of Carter's arms. Rested her head against his chest.

"Ellery?"

"Mmm-hmm?"

"Is this the forgiveness part? Or the second-chances part?"

"Both," Ellery whispered. "Because I'm falling in love with you, too."

Carter's arms tightened around her. "For the last twenty-four hours, I've been trying to come up with some grand gesture, like those guys in the movies, so you'd believe me," he admitted. "But the truth is, I'm not very good at romance—"

Ellery pressed a finger to his lips and gave him a teasing smile. "I guess we'll have to practice that, too."

"I guess we will."

She was still smiling when Carter's lips met hers in a kiss that celebrated the wonder of Christmas, new beginnings and the promise of tomorrow.

Epilogue

❧

"You're a natural at this, Ellery." Aiden gave her an approving nod. "Rich used to say I had river water instead of blood in my veins and I think you inherited it, too."

Ellery smiled at her twin and rested the canoe paddle on her lap, content to let the river set her course for the moment.

Aiden had knocked on her door when the sun was waking up and told Ellery to meet him by the river.

She'd been looking forward to this for months.

Two canoes were waiting by the riverbank, one with faded red flames flowing from bow to stern and the other one of Liam's vintage designs.

Aiden had introduced her to Ben and Jerry, a pair of mischievous otters, and entertained her with stories about River Quest. Ellery had seen the passion blazing in Aiden's eyes when he'd talked about modifications they would be making to next year's course so that people with disabilities could compete in the event.

Ellery hadn't said anything, but River Quest was the kind of project the Marshall Foundation could get behind. She made a mental note to talk to Phil. Two months ago, the woman had officially transitioned from housekeeper to full-time employee of the foundation.

Ellery knew her parents would approve.

She'd been driving back and forth all spring, but the more time she spent in Castle Falls, the more difficult it was to leave. She divided her time between Sunni's home and the inn. Two places where her favorite people in the world resided.

"That's Eagle Rock." Aiden pointed to a rock wall beyond the bend of the river. "We don't have time to climb it today."

"That's too bad."

Aiden saw right through her disappointed sigh and grinned. "I don't know about you, but I'm starving. Ready to head back?"

Ellery nodded.

Carter was working today, but her heart still lifted at the thought of spending some time with him and Bea at the end of his shift.

"Ready." She deliberately splashed Aiden with her paddle as she turned the canoe. When he ducked to avoid the spray, Ellery dug in and glided ahead of him.

"Race you!"

Ellery knew her twin would gain on her in a matter of seconds. She looked over her shoulder and realized he wasn't even trying. Ellery followed his gaze and her mouth dropped open.

Dozens of helium balloons lined the shoreline, swaying back and forth in time like colorful reeds. Interspersed among them were the people whose lives had become knit to Ellery's over the past few months.

Sunni stood beside Karen and…*Jameson*? The attorney had visited Castle Falls to meet Ellery's brothers right after the New Year. They'd won him over immediately, of course, and it was Jameson who'd convinced the director of the Holt-McIntyre Agency to turn over Ellery's file and share anything she knew about the family's history.

Carter had been seated at Ellery's side when she and her brothers found out that Carla and Darren Kane had been estranged when Ellery and Aiden were born. Darren had turned up several months later and convinced Carla to take him back, but she hadn't told him about Ellery. Just like she hadn't told Ray and Candace Marshall about Brendan and Liam, either. The couple had had no idea the infant girl they'd taken in had two older brothers as well as a twin.

It was bittersweet, finding out that her adoptive parents had, in fact, approached Carla about adopting Aiden, too. But their biological mother had been afraid of Darren's reaction and refused to consider it.

According to the director, Ray and Candace had lived in constant fear that Carla would change her mind and want Ellery back. Shortly before Carla signed the adoption papers, she and Darren Kane were arrested for drug possession.

When the Marshalls visited Carla in jail, not only did she insist on going ahead with a closed adoption, she made Candace and Ray promise they wouldn't tell Ellery anything about her biological family. Carla wanted Ellery to have the kind of opportunities she'd never been given.

Your parents took that promise as seriously as the one they made to love and care for you, the agency director had told Ellery.

Knowing that had given Ellery a sense of peace. So did knowing that God had brought the family together again.

"Wow." A grin broke across Aiden's face as he spotted Maddie in the middle of the throng gathered on the riverbank. The couple had set the date for an autumn wedding, a year from the day they'd officially met at the library.

Liam and Anna stood next to them, the twins at their side, jumping up and down. Brendan's arm was around Lily's waist, his hand resting on her rounded tummy.

They'd made the announcement a month ago, and everyone was thrilled there would be another addition to the family by next Christmas.

Joy washed over Ellery as she saw a dark-haired man and a little girl waving to her from the riverbank.

She twisted to face Aiden. "Did you know about this?"

"Not a clue," he said cheerfully. "But where there are balloons and people, there's usually cake. And ice cream."

His canoe shot ahead of hers, cutting through the water with barely a ripple. Ellery was laughing so hard she could barely keep up.

Her canoe scraped against the sandy bottom in the shallows and Carter was already there, reaching for her hand.

"Happy birthday."

Carter's whisper sent a shiver tumbling down Ellery's spine. She *was* happy.

Sunni had asked Ellery to come over for a cookout in honor of her and Aiden's twenty-sixth birthdays, but she'd never imagined the invitation had been extended to their friends and family.

"I thought you had to work today."

"My shift got changed." Carter paused. "Permanently."

"You transferred to the investigation unit? Why didn't you tell me?"

"I wanted to wait until it was official."

Ellery scooped Bea up in her arms. "This day is full of surprises."

Carter pressed a quick kiss against Ellery's temple.

"It isn't over yet."

Carter didn't mind sharing Ellery. He loved watching her interact with her brothers. Join in an impromptu game of tag with Bea and Anna's twins. Argue with Aiden over who should get the last piece of birthday cake.

But the party had ended a few hours ago and when they'd returned to the inn, the sun was setting over the pond. And Carter couldn't wait to be alone with Ellery.

"I think Bea and I will wander down to the barn and pay Sugar a visit," Karen announced, almost as if she'd read his mind.

Bea, who'd almost fallen asleep on the drive home, perked up at the words. "I'll get some carrots!"

She scampered from the room and Carter wondered if he'd imagined the sparkle in Karen's eyes before she followed.

He turned to Ellery. "Walk with me?"

She tucked her arm through his. "I thought you'd never ask."

They stepped outside and Carter steered her toward the orchard. The apple blossoms were in bloom, adding a touch of sweetness to the air.

He'd driven through minefields and never been this nervous.

Carter's fingers closed around the small velvet jewelry box in his pocket.

He'd wanted to propose to Ellery somewhere special. A place that marked the beginning of what Carter hoped, no, *prayed*, would be a lifetime together.

Earlier that morning, he'd been talking to God about Ellery and the future and felt what could only have been a divine tap on his shoulder. He'd looked out the window at the orchard. A reminder that something amazing could happen after a long winter, even the winter in a man's soul.

Carter stopped under the canopy of branches and Ellery looked at him quizzically.

"Is something wrong?"

"No…but I wanted to get this right."

Ellery's heart nearly stopped beating when Carter went down on one knee. He opened a small jewelry box, revealing a stunning princess-cut diamond.

"Will you marry me, Ellery? I want to spend the rest of my life with you. I want the sunrises and sunsets and everything in between. I know you found your brothers a few months ago, but I want us to be a family, too."

Ellery pressed her hand against her mouth. "Yes." She breathed the word. *"Yes."*

Carter slid the ring on her finger and planted a kiss on the inside of her wrist before he rose to his feet again.

Ellery launched herself into his arms and felt the steady thump of his heart against hers.

"I love you," Carter whispered. "Words can't describe how much."

She peeked up at him under her lashes. "Then maybe you should show me."

Carter's slow smile made Ellery's pulse skip. He bent his head and claimed her lips in a tender kiss filled with passion and promises and a lifetime of wishes that Ellery couldn't wait to come true.

When they finally broke apart, Carter looked a little dazed.

"Is tomorrow too soon for a wedding?" he asked.

"No," Ellery said promptly, making Carter laugh.

She loved to hear him laugh.

"Other people are going to weigh in on that decision, I have no doubt..." Carter paused. Shook his head. "And it looks like those people are here."

Ellery followed his gaze. Vehicles of all shapes and sizes were parked in front of the inn.

"Either the Tanners decided to show up a week early for their reunion," Carter said drily, "or we have a mole in the family."

Ellery laughed, knowing Carter's reaction was all for show.

"Two celebrations in one weekend." She wound her arms around his neck and planted another lingering kiss on his lips. "Do you think there's cake?"

Carter caught her hand, tucked it under his arm. "You've been hanging out with Aiden too much."

Everyone had gathered in the living room and Bea catapulted off the sofa when she saw them in the doorway.

"You're back!"

"And so is everyone else," Carter murmured.

Ellery nudged him with her elbow and dutifully held out her hand. The women crowded around them and Bea wriggled in between Sunni and Karen.

"I helped Daddy pick it out," she announced. "But I couldn't tell anyone 'cause it was a secret."

Aiden winked at Ellery. "We kept it a secret, too."

"You knew about this?"

"Carter asked for our blessing." Brendan worked his way into the circle and gave her a hug. "We haven't decided where he fits in the family hierarchy yet, though, have we, Liam?"

"Nope." Her middle brother shook Carter's hand and planted a kiss on Ellery's cheek.

Carter grinned, not the least bit intimidated by her brothers. "The only place I want to be is at Ellery's side."

Ellery smiled up at her future husband.

That sounded perfect to her, too.

* * * * *

*If you enjoyed this story,
look for the other Castle Falls books
by Kathryn Springer:*

The Bachelor Next Door
The Bachelor's Twins
The Bachelor's Perfect Match

Dear Reader,

At the beginning of the series, I had no idea that Ellery Marshall, the Kanes' missing sister, would end up with a story of her own. And of course it had to take place during Christmas, my favorite time of the year. And include a handsome, slightly Scrooge-like county deputy and his adorable five-year-old daughter.

Because sometimes it's the gifts we aren't expecting that turn out to be the most precious.

It's my prayer that, like Ellery and Carter, you find peace and joy in knowing that God has already given us the greatest gift of all. The gift of His son, Jesus.

I hope you enjoyed your visit to Castle Falls! Please drop by my website at kathrynspringer.com and say hello or check out my Facebook page at Facebook.com/kathrynspringerauthor.

Walk in joy,

Kathryn Springer

COMING NEXT MONTH FROM
Love Inspired®

Available October 15, 2019

THE CHRISTMAS COURTSHIP
by Emma Miller
Caught up in a scandal in her Amish community, Phoebe Miller moves to her cousin's farm in Delaware hoping for forgiveness and a fresh start. The last thing Phoebe expects is to fall for bachelor Joshua Miller. But can their love survive her secret?

HER AMISH CHRISTMAS CHOICE
Colorado Amish Courtships • by Leigh Bale
Inheriting a shop from her grandfather could solve all of Julia Rose's problems—if Martin Hostetler will renovate it. As an *Englischer*, romance with the Amish man is almost impossible, especially with her mother against it. But Martin and his faith are slowly starting to feel like home...

WESTERN CHRISTMAS WISHES
by Brenda Minton and Jill Kemerer
Homecomings bring love for two cowboys in these holiday novellas, where a woman gets more than she bargained for with a foster teen to care for and a handsome cowboy next door, and a bachelor finds an instant family with a single mom and her little girl.

THE TEXAN'S SURPRISE RETURN
Cowboys of Diamondback Ranch • by Jolene Navarro
Returning home with amnesia years after he was declared dead, Xavier De La Rosa is prepared to reconnect with family—but he's stunned to learn he has a wife and triplets. Can he recover his memory in time to reunite his family for Christmas?

HIS CHRISTMAS REDEMPTION
Three Sisters Ranch • by Danica Favorite
Injured at Christmastime, Erin Drummond must rely on her ex-husband's help caring for her nephews. But as they stay on the ranch together, can Erin and Lance find a way to put their tragic past behind them and reclaim their love?

HOMETOWN CHRISTMAS GIFT
Bent Creek Blessings • by Kat Brookes
The last person widow Lainie Dawson thought to ask for help with her troubled child is her brother's friend Jackson Wade—the man she once loved. But when her son bonds with Jackson and begins to heal, Lainie must confront her past—and future—with the man she never forgot.

LOOK FOR THESE AND OTHER LOVE INSPIRED BOOKS WHEREVER BOOKS ARE SOLD, INCLUDING MOST BOOKSTORES, SUPERMARKETS, DISCOUNT STORES AND DRUGSTORES.

LICNM1019

Get 4 FREE REWARDS!

We'll send you 2 FREE Books plus 2 FREE Mystery Gifts.

Love Inspired® books feature contemporary inspirational romances with Christian characters facing the challenges of life and love.

FREE
Value Over
$20

YES! Please send me 2 FREE Love Inspired® Romance novels and my 2 FREE mystery gifts (gifts are worth about $10 retail). After receiving them, if I don't wish to receive any more books, I can return the shipping statement marked "cancel." If I don't cancel, I will receive 6 brand-new novels every month and be billed just $5.24 for the regular-print edition or $5.99 each for the larger-print edition in the U.S., or $5.74 each for the regular-print edition or $6.24 each for the larger-print edition in Canada. That's a savings of at least 13% off the cover price. It's quite a bargain! Shipping and handling is just 50¢ per book in the U.S. and $1.25 per book in Canada.* I understand that accepting the 2 free books and gifts places me under no obligation to buy anything. I can always return a shipment and cancel at any time. The free books and gifts are mine to keep no matter what I decide.

Choose one: ☐ **Love Inspired® Romance**
Regular-Print
(105/305 IDN GNWC)

☐ **Love Inspired® Romance**
Larger-Print
(122/322 IDN GNWC)

Name (please print)

Address   Apt. #

City   State/Province   Zip/Postal Code

Mail to the Reader Service:
IN U.S.A.: P.O. Box 1341, Buffalo, NY 14240-8531
IN CANADA: P.O. Box 603, Fort Erie, Ontario L2A 5X3

Want to try 2 free books from another series? Call 1-800-873-8635 or visit www.ReaderService.com.

---

*Terms and prices subject to change without notice. Prices do not include sales taxes, which will be charged (if applicable) based on your state or country of residence. Canadian residents will be charged applicable taxes. Offer not valid in Quebec. This offer is limited to one order per household. Books received may not be as shown. Not valid for current subscribers to Love Inspired Romance books. All orders subject to approval. Credit or debit balances in a customer's account(s) may be offset by any other outstanding balance owed by or to the customer. Please allow 4 to 6 weeks for delivery. Offer available while quantities last.

Your Privacy—The Reader Service is committed to protecting your privacy. Our Privacy Policy is available online at www.ReaderService.com or upon request from the Reader Service. We make a portion of our mailing list available to reputable third parties that offer products we believe may interest you. If you prefer that we not exchange your name with third parties, or if you wish to clarify or modify your communication preferences, please visit us at www.ReaderService.com/consumerschoice or write to us at Reader Service Preference Service, P.O. Box 9062, Buffalo, NY 14240-9062. Include your complete name and address.

LI20

Surprise fatherhood, Southern charm and a heartwarming family Christmas—read on for a sneak peek at Low Country Christmas, *the conclusion to Lee Tobin McClain's Safe Haven series!*

Cash remembered coming out to Ma Dixie's place at Christmas time growing up. The contrast with his own foster family's home had been extreme. There, six themed Christmas trees were spread throughout the house, decorated perfectly by the commercial operation that brought them out each year and took them away after the holidays. That same company had wrapped garlands around the staircase and strung lights outside the house.

It had all been grand. He remembered being shocked and impressed his first year with the family, because it had been so different from the humble holidays back in Alabama. But he hadn't been allowed to invite his brothers over; too much noise and mess, his foster mother had always said. If he wanted to see them, he had to find a ride out to Ma Dixie's, which he had done frequently.

Here, Christmas really felt like Christmas.

He opened another box of ornaments, pulled out an angel made of hard plastic and handed it to Holly to place on the tree.

"Is this your tree topper, Ma?" Holly asked, holding it up.

"Yes, it is. I usually have Pudge put it up, but…could you do it, Cash, honey?"

He did, easily reaching the top of the small tree. "Is Pudge okay?" he asked Ma. "Is that why the place isn't decorated yet? He's too sick to help?"

Ma arranged the last figures in the Nativity scene and sank down onto the couch. "That's part of it. Mostly, it's me feeling blue. I'm not used to Christmas with no kids around."

Holly tilted her head to one side. "Did you have a lot of kids?"

"Dozens," Ma said with a wide smile. "That's the beauty of being a foster parent."

"Oh," Holly said as she sank down onto an ottoman beside Ma. "Do you…not foster anymore?"

Ma sighed. "I really can't with Pudge having all these doctor appointments. I guess maybe we're getting too old for it." She looked wistfully at the tree. "I just, you know, always enjoyed having the little ones around."

Holly looked thoughtful. "Is that why you wanted to take care of Penny? Not to help me out, but to have a little one around?"

"That's part of it," Ma said, "but don't you worry about it. I understand being picky where your child is concerned."

"It's not pickiness," Holly said. "If I were being picky, who better than an experienced foster parent like you?" She reached out and rubbed Ma's arm back and forth, two or three times, an affectionate gesture that made Ma smile.

Cash came over and sat at Holly's side, leaning against the ottoman. His heart, like that of the Grinch in the movie playing muted on the television, seemed to be expanding.

He'd taken plenty of women to high-end Christmas parties and fancy restaurants. But sitting here in Ma Dixie's house, talking with her about holidays and kids and family problems, decorating the tree with her, felt different. Like coming home.

Like coming home, with Holly beside him.

He put that feeling together with the questions his brother and Pudge had been asking. He was getting the horrifying notion that he might be falling in love with Holly. But he wasn't the falling-in-love type, or the settling-down type. And Holly wasn't the type for a short, superficial fling.

So what exactly was he going to do with all these feelings?

Don't miss Lee Tobin McClain's
Low Country Christmas,
available October 2019 from HQN Books!

Looking for inspiration in tales
of hope, faith and heartfelt romance?

Check out **Love Inspired**® and
Love Inspired® **Suspense** books!

New books available every month!

CONNECT WITH US AT:

Facebook.com/groups/HarlequinConnection

Facebook.com/HarlequinBooks

Twitter.com/HarlequinBooks

Instagram.com/HarlequinBooks

Pinterest.com/HarlequinBooks

ReaderService.com

SPECIAL EXCERPT FROM

Love Inspired®
SUSPENSE

*An NYPD officer's widow becomes the target of
her husband's killer. Can her husband's best friend
and his K-9 partner keep her safe and take the
murderer down once and for all?*

Read on for a sneak preview of
Sworn to Protect *by Shirlee McCoy,*
the exciting conclusion to the
True Blue K-9 Unit series, available
November 2019 from Love Inspired Suspense.

"Come in," Katie Jameson called, bracing herself for the meeting with Dr. Ritter.

The door swung open and a man in a white lab coat stepped in, holding her chart close to his face.

Only, he was not the doctor she was expecting.

Dr. Ritter was in his early sixties with salt-and-pepper hair and enough extra weight to fill out his lab coat. The doctor who was moving toward her had dark hair and a muscular build. His scuffed shoes and baggy lab coat made her wonder if he were a resident at the hospital where she would be giving birth.

"Good morning," she said. She had been meeting with Dr. Ritter since the beginning of the pregnancy. He understood her feelings about the birth. Talking about the fact that Jordan wouldn't be around for his daughter's birth, her childhood, her life always brought her close to the tears she despised.

"Morning," he mumbled.

"Is Dr. Ritter running late?" she asked, uneasiness joining the unsettled feeling in the pit of her stomach.

"He won't be able to make it," the man said, lowering the charts and grinning.

She went cold with terror.

She knew the hazel eyes, the lopsided grin, the high forehead. "Martin," she stammered.

"Sorry it took me so long to get to you, sweetheart. I had to watch from a distance until I was certain we could be alone."

"Watch?"

"They wanted to keep me in the hospital, but our love is too strong to be denied. I escaped for you. For us." He lifted a hand, and if she had not jerked back, his fingers would have brushed her cheek.

He scowled. "Have they brainwashed you? Have they turned you against me?"

"You did that yourself when you murdered my husband," she responded.

Don't miss
Sworn to Protect *by Shirlee McCoy,*
available November 2019 wherever
Love Inspired® Suspense books and ebooks are sold.

www.LoveInspired.com